Life
for
Lucy

Life
for
Lucy

Jenny Ashmole

The Book Guild Ltd

First published in Great Britain in 2021 by
The Book Guild Ltd
9 Priory Business Park
Wistow Road, Kibworth
Leicestershire, LE8 0RX
Freephone: 0800 999 2982
www.bookguild.co.uk
Email: info@bookguild.co.uk
Twitter: @bookguild

Copyright © 2021 Jenny Ashmole

The right of Jenny Ashmole to be identified as the author of this
work has been asserted by her in accordance with the
Copyright, Design and Patents Act 1988.

All rights reserved. No part of this publication may be
reproduced, transmitted, or stored in a retrieval system, in any form or by any means,
without permission in writing from the publisher, nor be otherwise circulated in
any form of binding or cover other than that in which it is published and without
a similar condition being imposed on the subsequent purchaser.

Typeset in 11pt Minion Pro

Printed on FSC accredited paper
Printed and bound in Great Britain by 4edge Limited

ISBN 978 1913913 625

British Library Cataloguing in Publication Data.
A catalogue record for this book is available from the British Library.

To my good friend Maureen
A true friend in need.

1

March

One windy day in March, Lucy climbed the steep rise of Light Street, where tall, slatey houses reared like grey cliffs against the sky. Nearly at the top of the hill she mounted a flight of wide stone steps up to one of the houses, with the name "Crimmond" on the fanlight above the blue front door. She climbed three flights of narrow stairs up to her attic flat, where she sat on the bed and pulled the local newspaper from her bag. Studying the entertainment section, she read: "*LUKE FINN AT THE RAILWAY FOLK CLUB TONIGHT*".

Luke Finn was an Irish folk singer who occasionally performed at the Railway folk club on Thursday evenings. He was Lucy's ideal of masculinity, with a subtle humour and a wicked twinkle in his eye… and unattainable, of course. Sometimes she indulged in fantasies where they met, and she'd be confident and sophisticated and know how to talk to him, though she knew she'd be struck dumb with shyness if they really met. She boiled an egg on the hotplate of a small electric stove, ate her tea and got ready to go out.

It was a chilly March evening. The sky was deepening to indigo, with the first faint stars appearing, and a blackbird sang cheerfully among the chimneys. Lucy felt elated by the cold wind and blackbird's song as she hurried down the hill to the lights of Redfold town.

The folk club was held in a big brown cave of a room at the Railway Hotel down by the station yard. Sometimes the thunder of passing diesel trains drowned the music. Lucy sat in the brown gloom, with one eye on the stage and one on the shadowed faces around her. She came here every week, partly to enjoy the music and partly in the hope of Meeting Someone. She was suddenly aware of a boy watching her from the next table, and her face stiffened. She tried to arrange her mouth in a half smile and put an animated sparkle in her eyes but couldn't keep it up. Then Luke Finn walked up on the stage, and Lucy forgot the boy.

Luke Finn was a darkly bearded Irishman in his thirties. He sang Irish rebel or love songs in his gritty voice, accompanied by a guitar, and sometimes he played reels on a banjo. For Lucy this banjo was a sexual symbol as he stood there, dark and virile, producing harsh, harmonious sounds from it. Yet while she enjoyed the music, its careless beat and subtle notes seemed to tease and torment her with suggestions of exciting erotic undercurrents in life, which were passing her by…

Her self-consciousness returned in a rush when Luke Finn left the stage, and Lucy was again aware of the boy watching her. He came over and asked, "Can I buy you a drink?"

Lucy pretended to start, as if suddenly aware of him, and smiled. "Yes, please."

"What will you have?"

"Eh... a ginger wine, please." She didn't like to ask for anything too expensive or too filling.

"I noticed you just now," he remarked when he returned with the drinks. "You look like you're enjoying yourself."

"Yes," she replied, "I like this kind of music."

Screening her mouth with her glass, Lucy took a good look at him, and was disappointed. He was quite young – only about eighteen, she guessed – with a shiny face, sandy hair and spectacles. *Well*, she decided, *I'd better be nice to him, he might be alright in spite of his looks.*

"I'm Bob Hicks," he introduced himself.

The name "Mrs Lucy Hicks" flashed involuntarily in her mind's eye...

"I'm Lucy Grey," she replied.

"That's a nice name," he observed vaguely, then they listened in silence to the next singer.

They walked back together afterwards, and Bob asked, "What do you do?"

"I'm a secretary."

"Whereabouts?"

"Ministry of Agriculture."

"Oh... do you like it?"

"Not particularly," she answered, a bit irritated. "It's just a job."

"I'm an apprentice technician at the hospital," he told her. She let him hold her hand as they walked. It would seem silly to refuse, but she didn't like his hand's damp, fishy feel and wished she could politely drop it.

"Are you doing anything tomorrow night?" Bob asked after a while.

"No."

"Shall we go dancing at the Mecca?" he suggested.

Lucy hated the Mecca ballroom. It was lush, flashy and vulgar, like a jungle of gaudy lights, steamy bodies and loud, pounding music. But she found herself replying, "Yes alright then," even though she knew she didn't much like this boy and probably wouldn't enjoy tomorrow evening at all. She just didn't like to let a chance slip, however unlikely it seemed at first.

"I'll meet you here outside the Odeon at eight, if that's okay." He waved goodbye. "Cheerio, I've got to catch a bus now." He disappeared across the road.

*

The sun woke Lucy next morning, beaming through the skylight window. She lay listening to the scratchings and cooings of pigeons on the roof tiles, feeling cheerful. She loved this little attic flat, with its sloping ceiling and skylight window.

Then she remembered that it was her birthday. *Twenty-three*, she reflected, *and nothing much to show for it.* In her teens she'd looked forward to her twenties as a time when she'd be everything she wanted to be – confident, sophisticated, married with children and perhaps with a book or two published. Yet here she was at twenty-three, just as awkward and immature as she'd been at eighteen.

She got out of bed and looked in the mirror. She knew she was pretty, with big dreamy blue-grey eyes that were rather short-sighted, and soft light brown hair nestling on her shoulders. *Why aren't men interested in me?* she wondered, staring at herself. She knew why really: it was because she was too reserved and awkward in her manner; it made people feel uncomfortable with her.

She desperately longed to be married, partly for status, partly for the unknown excitement of sex and romance, and partly for the security of knowing that – whatever the rest of the world thought of her – there'd be one person who'd think enough of her to want to spend his life with her.

Lucy got dressed, then went down to collect the milk and mail. There were a few cards for her and a parcel from her parents. She opened it as she sat eating cornflakes at the white wooden table beneath the skylight. It was a book of old folk songs that she'd once casually mentioned to her father, and he'd remembered.

Lucy smiled, then sighed, feeling guilty that her father thought of her and studied her interests, while she seldom thought of or bothered to write to him. She felt it a burden that he was fond of her and worried about her. *But then,* she reflected, *that's how life is – parents give and children take, until they become parents themselves and give to their children, and so it goes on.*

She knew she'd disappointed her parents by not taking up a professional career. Armed with two A levels at eighteen, she'd followed her father's suggestion that she become a librarian, as she "liked books". She soon discovered that liking books was only part of library work. She found it stressful dealing with the public, and library theory was very boring, all about cataloguing and classification.

So, not sure what to do next, she did a course in shorthand and typing at evening classes, then got a job as a secretary in a solicitors' office. Here she complicated matters by falling in love with one of her bosses, a pleasant, good-humoured young man called Samuel. As soon as Lucy realised her feelings for Samuel, it made her painfully shy and abrupt with him. She just didn't know how to behave with a man whom she liked. She desperately wanted to attract and encourage him but knew helplessly that she repelled him instead by her manner.

Looking back on it, she wondered whether she'd really loved him, or was it just that she was all geared up to fall in love with someone anyway, and it happened to be Samuel who was there? But it had seemed real enough at the time, and she'd been very unhappy when she realised he didn't return her feelings. Eventually he got engaged to another girl.

Devastated, Lucy decided to leave the little Cornish town where she'd lived twenty-two years. She studied newspaper advertisements and found a secretarial job in the Civil Service at Redfold in Surrey. It was a complete change from the West Country, but not too far away, so she could visit home three times a year, at Christmas, Easter and in the summer.

She'd been in this job at Redfold a year now. *It's not a particularly interesting job*, reflected Lucy as she walked down Light Street to the bus stop by the Odeon cinema, but she was content there and had a lot of odd moments when there wasn't much work to do, so she sat at her desk writing stories when no-one was looking. She was still young enough to imagine herself writing a really wonderful book one day that would make her famous, though she had no idea what this book would be about.

Standing at the bus stop, the sight of the Odeon cinema reminded Lucy that she'd be meeting that boy there tonight. She grimaced, wondering whether to bother after all.

"Cheer up, love!" called a passing workman on his bicycle. Lucy scowled at his retreating back. She knew her face had a woebegone look when she was thinking, even when her thoughts weren't miserable. *Oh no*, she reflected as the big green bus loomed up the hilly High Street, *they'll know it's my birthday at work, they always know everyone's birthday, and I won't know what to say...*

It was just a short bus ride to the Ministry of Agriculture buildings, situated between a busy main road and a golf course. Lucy worked mostly for Charlie Radlett, a plump, jovial young executive officer who was working on a project to convert chicken manure into cattle food. He kept pellets of it in polythene bags in the filing cabinet. Lucy wasn't in the least attracted to him, nor he to her, but she felt awkward and ill at ease with him just because he was a man and of her own generation. *Sex is a nuisance*, she thought. *It stops me being natural with men and seeing them just as people.* Charlie sensed this reserve in his secretary, which made him uncomfortable with her too. Lucy knew that even if she worked there for the next ten years they'd always be just as awkward with each other.

She was more at ease with older men. Sometimes she typed letters for a big jolly Yorkshireman called George Riley. He came into the office as she was opening Charlie's post.

"Ah, here's our little Lucy," he greeted her breezily in his fat Yorkshire voice. "Happy birthday! I bet you'll be celebrating with a boyfriend tonight, eh? Ha ha!"

Lucy wished she didn't blush so easily. Mr Riley's bantering irritated her, but she didn't know how to carry it off coolly, as he well knew.

Among the post was a birthday card for her from all the clerical staff in the department, a group of middle-aged women and young girls. The women gossiped about illnesses, their husbands and the price of food, while the girls chattered about clothes and boyfriends. Lucy sat in her corner feeling sour and superior – sour because she didn't know how to join in their chatter and superior because it was trivial anyway. Her father had a name for such people whose minds didn't rise much above television, shopping and playing bingo: he called them "bingo people". Yet they had what Lucy had not – companionship with each other and freedom from the introverted self-consciousness that made life so difficult for her.

But she had her compensations. During lunch hours she liked to wander along by the golf course, planning stories. Even though she'd given up trying to get them published, the creating and writing of them gave her intense pleasure. *Those bingo women know nothing of that*, reflected Lucy, *for all their superficial contentment with life... I suppose I'd better thank them for the birthday card.* She waited for a gap in their chatter, and several times almost plucked up courage to speak, then didn't, then missed her chance. Eventually the tea lady came round, so while they all queued up Lucy said awkwardly to the nearest one, "Thank you for the birthday card."

"You're welcome," beamed a large motherly lady called Mrs Browning. "How old are you now, twenty-one?"

"No, a bit more than that!" Lucy tried to laugh lightly.

"Are you doing anything nice tonight?" asked Mrs Browning.

"No," replied Lucy shortly. She saw one of the girls looking at her curiously and wondered if she was thinking her weird, then returned to her desk and sat sipping her tea, trying to concentrate on the letter she was typing.

It was a perfect day for a walk in the lunch hour. The turf lay smooth as green suede, and larks hung twittering in the clear blue sky. Lucy's spirits rose, and she persuaded herself that she might enjoy the evening with that boy after all.

At half past seven that evening Lucy put on a blue corduroy dress and a splash of pink lipstick, then regarded her face critically in the mirror. Apart from a faint line between her eyebrows, her face was as young and smooth as at eighteen, and it always pleased her when people thought her younger than she was. *It's a nuisance having to go out*, she thought suddenly. *It would have been pleasant spending a quiet evening browsing through my new book.* Still, she couldn't just not turn up and leave the poor boy hanging about outside the Odeon.

She arrived there just before eight o'clock, trying to remember what he'd looked like. The steps in front of the Odeon were empty. Lucy frowned and glanced at her watch. Maybe he'd missed the bus and was catching a later one. Ten minutes later a bus sailed over the hill and down to the Odeon bus stop. Lucy watched as the passengers spilled out, but there was no sandy-haired boy in glasses. Still she waited, trying to look nonchalant and unconcerned. A couple of youths clumped by, calling waggishly, "He's not comin', darlin'!"

By twenty past eight Lucy faced the fact that Bob Hicks wasn't turning up. Either he'd forgotten, been detained or just couldn't be bothered. It had happened to her before, but each time she felt just as bitter and humiliated. She turned and trudged back up Light Street. The black sky was speckled with stars, and halfway up the hill she turned to view the lights of Redfold, glittering like cold yellow diamonds. A pair of lovers stumbled past her in the darkness, laughing and whispering together. *Why can't I be like that with someone?* thought Lucy bitterly. *Why have I got this cussed awkward personality that won't let me make relationships with people?*

Slowly she climbed the steps up to Crimmond's front door and up to her attic, irritated that she couldn't enjoy a quiet evening in, now that it had been so disrupted. She heated up a pan of milk, made a mug of weak coffee and curled up on the bed. Feeling too churned up to read, she switched on the radio. "All Kinds of Everything…" sang a girl's clear sweet voice. It was the song that had won the Eurovision Song contest that year, 1970. Lucy liked it; it was more like a folk song than a pop song, with its lilting melody. She relaxed and sipped her coffee, letting the music wash over her while she idly studied the faded pink roses on the wallpaper.

2

April

Lucy woke one Sunday morning and lay listening to April rain drumming on the skylight window. It was just light enough for the grey roses to show up on the wall, and the mirror gleamed faintly in the dimness. There was something she'd made up her mind to do today... *Ah yes*, she remembered. The room grew lighter, so she sat up and pushed back the blue flowery quilt, reaching for yesterday's local newspaper on the chair. Turning to the personal column, she read an advertisement: "*Young man aged twenty-eight would like to meet girl for friendship. Matrimony if suited. Any age.*"

Lucy smiled at the "any age" bit, wondering if any older women had taken him literally. She had often contemplated answering one of these advertisements, or even joining a marriage bureau, then decided against it. It would be like applying for a job, no romance in it at all, just sizing each other up as a possible husband or wife.

She washed her face at the chipped enamel sink, ate her cornflakes, then wrote a letter to the advertisement's box number. Suddenly aware of an increase of light in the room, she looked up to see that the sky was now swept clean and blue. By standing on the chair she could open the skylight window and look out.

The rain had cleared to a fine April morning. The red roofs of Redfold glowed warm in the sunshine, and in the distance Lucy could view the blue hills of Hampshire. She liked being up there among the chimneys and television aerials, and the distant chime of church bells. It all made her feel suddenly alive and in the centre of things…

"Lucy!" called a voice at the door. "Are you in?"

Lucy scrambled down from the chair, letting the window fall shut with a crash. She opened the door to Ruth, the girl from the other attic flat across the passage.

"What was that?" Ruth's bright inquisitive eyes darted around the room. "Did I make you drop something?"

"No, it's alright," replied Lucy nervously. "It was only the window."

Ruth was about twenty, very attractive with long auburn hair and sharp green eyes. She worked in a bank in the town. Whenever Lucy met anyone intelligent and educated, as this girl obviously was, she had an aggressive desire to show that she was just as good as them, despite her provincial accent. This desire made her manner more nervous than usual.

Ruth strolled in and sat in the lumpy yellow armchair. "I just dropped in to ask if you could lend me some sugar," she explained. "I've run out."

"Yes, of course." Lucy poured some sugar into the carton that Ruth provided, spilling some of it on the table.

Ruth watched her with cool, amused eyes, then stretched and yawned, grumbling, "I feel awful this morning, Bill and I went to a party last night and now I've got a splitting headache."

Not sure how to reply, Lucy mumbled, "Oh."

"Do you go out much?" asked Ruth curiously.

"Not a lot," replied Lucy. "Well, I go to the Railway folk club sometimes."

"Who with?"

"By myself," answered Lucy. "I go to listen to the music there."

"Of course, why else? I'll take you to a party sometime," offered Ruth. "Thanks for the sugar. Bye."

When Ruth had gone, Lucy sat at the table and sighed, knowing she'd been clumsy and awkward. She admired and envied Ruth, who had so much more confidence than herself. Maybe she'd have more confidence if she had a boyfriend. She knew Ruth had a boyfriend who often stayed the night with her. Sometimes Lucy lay awake in her own virginal bed and pictured what was going on in the bed in the room across the passage, clenching her teeth in the darkness. She had a gnawing curiosity about sex. Wherever she went, wherever she looked, she couldn't get away from it. It screamed at her from cinema boards and newspapers; it leered at her in the songs at the Railway folk club. Lucy felt ashamed of still being a virgin at twenty-three. She knew that most of the world shared this exciting secret of sex from which she was excluded, and felt a dull anger at the fact that she hadn't kept her virginity from choice but because she'd never had a chance to lose it. She knew that if someone like Luke Finn took notice of her, then she'd want to lie down and let him do what he liked with her. If Luke Finn hadn't been married, she might have tried somehow to approach him, but she supposed that once a man was married he lost all interest in other women.

She wondered what to do until lunchtime. Oh yes, she'd write in her diary. She pulled out a tin box from under the bed, unlocked it and took out a bound blank book half full of writing. Lucy's diary was like a friend to her, she poured out all her hopes and fears and frustrations into its pages.

About an hour later Lucy fried two sausages for lunch on the electric hotplate. Then she went out to post her letter. She waited nearly a week for a reply. On the following Saturday morning there was a letter in her pigeon-hole in the hall. She frowned at the writing on the envelope; it was decidedly "bingo", being angular and childish. The letter was badly written and mis-spelt on a sheet of lined paper:

"Dear Lucy, thankyou for your leter. Can I meet you outside Woolworths sat eve at 7:30. Yours sincerly, John Loat."

Mrs Lucy Loat, thought Lucy. *No, I don't like that!* She could tell by his letter that they wouldn't be at all suited. He hadn't even given her a chance to say if she was free to meet him that evening. *Well*, she decided, *I'll go anyway...*

Life *for* Lucy

*

When she was ready that evening, Lucy climbed up on the chair and peered out of the skylight. The sun was shining, but the town's roofs glowed orange against an inky sky. *I suppose I'd better take the umbrella*, she decided with irritation. She was wearing her new blue linen jacket that she didn't want to get wet, but she knew she'd find the umbrella a nuisance if it didn't rain. In the end she took it.

As Lucy walked down Light Street the sky cleared to a fine spring evening. *Damn!* she fumed. *There's no time to go back and dump the umbrella now.* Walking down Redfold High Street, she was dismayed to see one of the women from work just in front of her. It was Mrs Browning, sauntering along and pausing at shop windows as if she had all the time in the world. Lucy lurked in a doorway for a few minutes, but Mrs Browning didn't progress very far. *I could have taken the umbrella back after all*, thought Lucy crossly, *the time I'm wasting here.* Suddenly Mrs Browning looked behind her just as Lucy emerged from the doorway.

"Hello, Lucy," she called. "Where are you off to?"

"Just going to see someone," replied Lucy.

"I'll ask my husband to give you a lift," suggested Mrs Browning. "I'm meeting him at the bottom of the High Street in five minutes."

"No, don't bother," protested Lucy. "I'm not going far, only just past Woolworths."

"I'll walk down with you." At a maddeningly slow

April

pace they walked down past Woolworths, where Lucy saw a figure lurking, then she left Mrs Browning and shot up a side street that took her back near Woolworths in a roundabout way. Outside Woolworths stood a large young man with pale blue eyes and springy hair.

"Are you Mr John Loat?" asked Lucy hesitantly.

"Yes, I am." His face broke into a smile. "I was beginning to think you'd let me down, like."

"I didn't mean to be late," apologised Lucy. "I met someone I know and couldn't get away in time."

John Loat seemed pleased with his first impression of Lucy, and suggested, "Shall we go for a drink at the Green Man?"

"Yes, alright," agreed Lucy.

They walked through the park in silence, where tulips glowed red and yellow in the evening sunlight.

"How old are you?" asked John suddenly.

"Twenty-three," she replied, disappointed when he didn't remark how young she looked for her age.

In the rather flashy plush saloon of the Green Man, Lucy kicked her umbrella under the table and decided to break the ice by asking, as they sat with their drinks, "What made you put an advert in the paper?"

"Well," he grinned, "I was engaged once, yer see, but she broke it off and went in the army. Then the fellas at work dared me to put an advert in the paper for another girlfriend. What made you answer?"

"Well," muttered Lucy, not sure what to say, "I get a bit lonely sometimes…" She sipped her ginger wine to make it last a long time, so that she had something to occupy her hands and mouth.

"I got a reply from a girl of thirty," continued John. "We went out last night, but we weren't suited, like. We just sat here saying nothing all evening."

Well, we're doing better than that, thought Lucy. *At least we're managing to say something.*

"I got two other replies and wrote to them," he went on, "but they didn't write back."

"Maybe they were put off by your handwriting!" suggested Lucy.

"Eh?" He looked at her blankly. "What's wrong with it?"

"Nothing," said Lucy hastily, "I was only joking."

Noticing that he'd finished his drink, she drained the last drop in her glass. He immediately asked, "Would you like another?"

"No, thanks… well, alright then, same again." She realised it was still only eight o'clock.

John went on to tell her all about his job as a bus driver, confiding that he planned to join the Merchant Navy soon. Lucy grew bored and began worrying what to do with her face. She kept thinking, *Shall I smile now? Shall I look away for a second? I can feel my mouth drooping; I hope I'm not going to blush!* And so on.

He stopped abruptly and asked, "Am I talking too much?"

"No, no," said Lucy hurriedly. "I… I like listening."

She declined a third drink, and they walked back through the park in the April dusk. Scents of cherry blossom hung in the air, and a blackbird sang sweetly.

April

Lucy wished she could be alone to enjoy it. Suddenly John made a lunge at her, muttering, "Give us a kiss."

Lucy pushed him off crossly. She didn't feel like it, not with him. She knew he was just trying to force their intimacy. They walked on in awkward silence, then John asked, "Was I too forward just now?"

Lucy hesitated, then explained, "It's just that I can't feel attracted to you until I know you better. What's the point of kissing someone I'm not attracted to? I wouldn't enjoy it."

"Oh." He looked puzzled.

Reaching the top of Light Street, Lucy paused outside Crimmond and lied, "I can't ask you in, the landlady's a bit fussy." The truth was that she didn't want to risk Ruth seeing him. Well, she wouldn't mind her seeing him but didn't want her to hear him speak.

"Shall we go out again tomorrow night?" asked John uncertainly.

"Well..." Lucy knew it would be hopeless to try to continue with him, but she found herself saying, "Alright then. Where shall we go?"

"For a drink again. Same time, same place?"

"Yes. Goodbye."

As Lucy climbed the stairs, she remembered that she'd left her umbrella under the table at the Green Man.

*

John was late turning up outside Woolworths next evening, and Lucy began to wonder if he'd backed out. At twenty to eight he came running up, saying breathlessly, "Sorry I'm late, Lu."

Rather annoyed at his shortening of her name, Lucy walked to the Green Man with him again, where she recovered her umbrella. He seemed preoccupied, until they finished their drinks and he suggested, "Would you like to come and see my flat?"

"Alright then." Lucy wondered why on earth she was agreeing. She didn't think he'd try to get her into bed; he was too clumsy to be a good seducer. Much as Lucy wanted to experience sex, she didn't want it with just anyone. She knew it would be pointless with someone she wasn't attracted to. She wondered if she was being too fussy, then reflected: *No, sex isn't just a physical thing; you must be able to communicate with the person you're doing it with, but this man and I live in different worlds, almost.*

John Loat lived in a ground-floor flat in one of the big houses off the main road. The red-brick house glowed like Cheshire cheese in the evening sunlight. A cedar tree in the front garden made his flat very shadowy. Lucy looked around the large room, then noticing the lack of any cooking facilities, she asked, "How do you cook your food?"

"There's a café down the road," he explained. "I have all my meals there."

"What, even breakfast?"

"Yeah, they know me there now, I have eggs and bacon every morning."

"Blimey!" exclaimed Lucy, amazed. One of her pleasures of living in a flat was getting her own meals when and how she liked.

"Give us a kiss, Lu," said John suddenly, clutching at her. "Don't be shy."

"I'm *not* shy," burst out Lucy in exasperation. "I just don't want your mouth on mine. I told you before, I wouldn't like it."

"Look here." He was sullen. "I know I vote Labour, but I'm quite clean and decent."

"So do I!" Lucy laughed. "Vote Labour, I mean… I'll go home now, there's a programme on the radio I want to listen to."

"Okay, I'll walk you back."

He seemed lost in thought as they walked, then, halfway up Light Street, he suddenly stopped and announced, "I won't be seeing yer no more, Lu. I don't think we're suited, like."

"No, neither do I," retorted Lucy, annoyed that he'd said it first.

"Cheerio, then," said John awkwardly.

"Goodbye," said Lucy coolly. As she walked up the hill she released her feelings in silent laughter, both at him and at herself. He'd probably go and tell "the fellas at work" how he'd met this prudish girl who wouldn't let him kiss her.

The dusk was softly grey-blue, with a wafer of new moon in the sky. Lucy felt free again. It was better to stay alone than go out with someone she didn't care for. Her attic seemed to welcome her as she went in and switched on the light. She made a mug of milky coffee, selected a book from the shelf and curled up on the bed with it. Pigeons scratted on the roof above, and an owl hooted among the chimneys.

3

May

One morning in May Lucy was walking to work across the golf course, which she liked to do on sunny days in spring and summer instead of getting the bus. The dewy turf was speckled with daisies, and hawthorn hedges were crusted white with blossom. She watched her feet make bluish trails in the damp turf and heard bees humming in the hedges. The weather always affected her spirits, so she felt cheerful this morning.

Then she remembered something and sighed. A complication had arisen at work: a man had joined the staff recently, and Lucy felt attracted to him. He was a Welshman called Mr Roberts, about forty, with dark greying hair and twinkling blue eyes. He was married, of course – attractive older men always were. He didn't actually work in Lucy's department but sometimes came in to chat to Charlie Radlett. Whenever Mr Roberts entered the room Lucy blushed hotly and made mistakes on her typewriter. He was well aware of this and played up to it.

The red-brick Ministry buildings glowed in the morning sunshine as Lucy approached them. She neither liked nor hated the place; she just felt indifferent to it. She'd never felt that she belonged or fitted there, but she wasn't unhappy there.

She sat at her desk and opened the mail.

Charlie Radlett came bouncing in and beamed. "Good morning!"

"Good morning." Lucy gave him her usual polite smile. They always started the day on these cordial terms but never grew any easier with each other. While Charlie was dictating some letters to her, Mr Roberts appeared.

"Hello, Charlie; hello, Lucy," he greeted them.

Lucy answered him but dared not look up. Her cheeks grew hot and her hand stiffened as she tried to carry on scribbling shorthand. Mr Roberts chatted to Charlie for a while, then turned to her and asked, in his soft Welsh voice, "How's our little Lucy this morning?"

"Alright, thanks," grunted Lucy, putting paper into her typewriter.

It stuck halfway, and Mr Roberts grinned. "I'd better disappear, I seem to have an adverse effect on Lucy; she starts doing everything wrong!"

"Ah, she fancies you!" said Charlie jocularly. He was able to be familiar to her when someone else was there. The two men laughed, and Lucy started jabbing furiously at her typewriter until they'd left the room.

Deciding to go and look for a file to hide her face for a while, she retreated behind one of the filing cabinets, then backed out again, muttering, "Sorry." One of the girls was adjusting her tights there. *Is there nowhere to hide?* fumed Lucy as she returned to her desk.

She calmed down after a while and idly flicked through yesterday's local newspaper that Charlie had left on his desk. She couldn't resist turning to the personal column, where her eye caught an advertisement: "*Gentleman aged thirty requires intelligent, imaginative young lady aged twenty-five to thirty. View friendship, matrimony if suited.*"

He sounds rather pompous, thought Lucy, *but at least he'll be different from John Loat.*

Back in her attic that evening she decided to try again, but if this one didn't work out she definitely wouldn't answer any more advertisements. She wrote:

> "*Dear sir, I saw your advertisement in the Redfold News and would like to meet you. I hope I am intelligent, though my age falls a bit short of your requirements, being only twenty-three, but I have plenty of imagination! I am free any evening.*"

She didn't have to wait long for a reply; it came by return of post, from a village called Hedgham a couple of miles out of Redfold. The handwriting was small and neat, and the letter ran:

> "*Dear Miss Grey, Thank you for your letter, I would be pleased to meet you. I will call for you at your*

May

house at 8pm on Friday evening and take you out for a drink. Yours sincerely, Brian Hobden."

Forgetting the possibility of being Mrs Lucy Hobden, she felt annoyed that he'd arranged to call at Crimmond. For all he knew, it might be awkward for her, though she didn't mind, really, unless he didn't look much good and Ruth might happen to see him.

*

Ruth knocked on the door on Friday evening just as Lucy was about to get ready to go out. "Lucy," she called. "Are you going out?"

"No," lied Lucy nervously, opening the door. "That is, I might, I'm not sure yet."

"That sounds suspicious!" Ruth laughed. "Bill and I are going to a party tonight, and I wondered if you'd like to come."

"Well," Lucy floundered, "I'd like to, really, but I can't... I'd like to come another time, though."

"Alright, I'll ask you again next time. Have a nice evening."

Lucy changed hurriedly into her blue corduroy dress and linen jacket, then left at ten to eight, lurking by a wall further up the road and hoping that Ruth and her boyfriend didn't leave for their party at the same time that Brian Hobden arrived.

At exactly eight o'clock a small white car drew up outside Crimmond, and a short, stocky man got out.

Lucy walked back quickly, approaching him just as he was climbing the steps. "Are you Mr Hobden?" she called.

He turned quickly. Lucy didn't like his face much; it was sallow and thickset, with dark hair standing up like a brush. But his grey eyes were serious and kindly. "Yes, I am," he said stiffly. "Are you Miss Lucy Grey, by any chance?"

"Yes," Lucy was relieved, "I didn't want you to ring the bell, so I waited out here."

"Oh. Would you care for a drink?"

"Yes, please." She climbed into the car quickly before Ruth should appear. Brian drove down to the Star pub, which pleased Lucy. It wasn't a flashy pub, like the Green Man, but a squat old timbered house, quiet and brown inside. She asked for the usual ginger wine, while Brian had a beer.

"What are your interests?" he asked her as they sat in the wooden alcove.

"Writing and folk music," replied Lucy, feeling as if she were attending an interview.

"Oh. What do you write?"

"Stories and poems."

"Have you ever been published?"

"No."

A short silence, then Brian said, "My hobby is wireless, I like constructing radios and things. I work at RDE." He named a technical firm that Lucy vaguely knew had a large works just outside the town. "What do you do for a job?" he asked.

"I'm a secretary in the Civil Service," answered Lucy, "at the Ministry of Agriculture."

Another silence, then Lucy, in an attempt to make things easier, asked, "What made you put an advert in the paper?"

It worked, and Brian loosened up a bit as he told her, "I've had a terrible job finding a steady girlfriend. I was working in the Air Force up in the Shetland Islands until recently, and there wasn't much choice up there!"

"Did you get any other replies?"

"I had one from a widow of fifty-nine, but I ignored it. I don't want a divorcee, either."

"Why not?"

"Well," he looked uncomfortable, "there's something I don't like about them, and the family wouldn't like it." His next question was, "What are your views on marriage?"

"Well…" Lucy hesitated, not sure what to say. "It's necessary, I suppose. Children need a father."

"Yes. Still, there's no point in forcing the issue… Brr, it's chilly in here suddenly."

Lucy couldn't help laughing at his abrupt change of subject.

His grey eyes regarded her with a puzzled expression. "Did I say something funny?" he asked.

"No, no." Lucy cast about desperately for something to say. "You, er… you live at Hedgham, don't you? That's a very pretty village, I went through it on the bus once."

"Yes, it's quite nice," he agreed. "I live there with my mother."

"Oh."

"Do you like cooking?" was his next question.

"Not particularly," replied Lucy. "I've got a grotty little

stove in my flat that takes ten minutes to boil a pan of milk, so I can't cook much."

They finished their drinks, then Brian suggested, "Would you like to come and have tea with my mother tomorrow afternoon?"

"Yes, alright then," answered Lucy doubtfully, not relishing the thought of meeting his mother.

Brian drove her back up Light Street, arranged to collect her outside the Odeon the following afternoon, then bade her goodbye as stiffly as he'd greeted her.

Lucy sat in her armchair with a contemplative cup of coffee. She didn't feel very optimistic about Brian Hobden. He was reserved, just as reserved as her in a different way. She suspected that he had no sense of humour, and his pomposity wasn't just shyness – he really was like that. He probably had the same problems as her in getting on with people. She wondered whether they'd be able to help each other at all.

*

Saturday dawned blue and sunny. Lucy was awakened by morning sunshine beaming through the skylight, and sparrows chattering among the chimneys. She stretched, wallowing in the warmth of her bed, studying the pink roses on the wallpaper. She wasn't sure whether or not she was looking forward to the afternoon. She wished she didn't have to meet his mother; it was too soon.

After she'd eaten her cornflakes, Lucy got ready to go out and buy food for the weekend. She wondered if she ought to buy some flowers for Brian's mother. She shied away from it; she didn't think she intended to become Mrs Hobden's daughter-in-law... but after all, the woman was giving her tea... In the end she bought a bunch of pink and purple anemones in the Saturday street market.

She was glad it wasn't raining; it would have been awkward managing her umbrella, handbag and the flowers. Deciding it was warm enough for a summer dress, she put on a flowery mauve cotton one.

At nearly three o'clock Lucy walked down Light Street, where fleecy young beech leaves hung over a brick wall near the main road, glowing so intensely green they seemed almost luminous. Brian was waiting for her outside the Odeon.

"Hello." He smiled shyly as she climbed into the car's front seat. "I was a bit early."

"Does your mother mind me coming?" asked Lucy as they sped along the road.

"Oh no," replied Brian. "She'll be pleased to meet you."

"Did you tell her how we met?"

"Good Lord, no! She didn't ask, anyway."

Soon they dipped down into Hedgham, a pretty thatched village nestling in downland.

"Could we walk around the village first?" suggested Lucy. "It's so pretty, I'd like to have a look round."

"Okay." Brian parked the car by the church. It was a little stone church with an ivy-clad tower. Its graveyard lay green and quiet in the afternoon sunshine.

"Do you go to church?" asked Lucy, curious as to his beliefs.

"Sometimes," he sounded annoyed. "Asking how often one goes to church is like asking how often one has a bath."

Lucy felt snubbed and disappointed. She would have liked to ask him about his religious beliefs and philosophy, perhaps leading to an interesting discussion. Looking around at the mossy gravestones, she remarked, "I'd rather be cremated than buried."

"Good Lord, what a subject to bring up!" exclaimed Brian.

Lucy decided they'd better leave the churchyard; it didn't seem to agree with them. "Let's go for a walk up that path." She pointed to a stile by a stone wall. "It looks inviting."

They wandered through a meadow spread yellow with buttercups, past lacey hawthorns and chestnut trees with cream cones of blossom. "You're lucky to live here," said Lucy. "It's beautiful. Do you walk up here much?"

"No. When one lives in a place one doesn't bother much about it."

Lucy thought of her hometown in Cornwall, how she loved to walk on the hills above it and by the sea below it. *This man is arid*, she reflected. *He has no soul.*

Eventually she couldn't put off meeting his mother any longer, and they approached one of the thatched cottages in the village street. It was very pretty and quaint, with diamond-paned windows and a perfectly neat little garden, sweet with the scent of lilac from a tree in purple bloom.

Mrs Hobden met them at the door. She was a short, plump lady with neat grey hair and steel-rimmed spectacles. She greeted Lucy stiffly but not unkindly, and shook her hand, Lucy quickly transferring the flowers to her left hand. "I thought you might like these anemones," she said nervously, handing over the bunch, its stem paper hot from her hand.

"Thank you, they're lovely." Mrs Hobden seemed pleased, and Lucy felt she'd done the right thing.

"How do you like Hedgham?" asked Mrs Hobden.

Lucy stammered a correct reply, recognising the look in Mrs Hobden's eyes that she often saw in people when confronted by her nervous manner for the first time. They either looked faintly amused or coldly puzzled. This woman looked the latter.

The cottage was neat and bright inside, furnished in mauve and sea-green.

"Would you like to see the stereo I made?" asked Brian, opening a gleaming wood cabinet. He enthused over its technicalities, which Lucy didn't understand, and she realised that here was Brian's soul – in wires and knobs and electric plugs. *How different we are*, she thought sadly. *What's the use of trying to go on with it?*

They ate dainty little sandwiches and cakes for tea in the dining room. The conversation lagged a bit, and Lucy wished she could go home soon. She felt she had no right to sit in this woman's house eating her food, when she intended to drop her son as soon as the evening was over.

"There's a fourteenth-century pub in the village," announced Brian after tea. "Shall we go there for a drink later on?"

"Yes, alright then," agreed Lucy, wondering how they'd fill in the time until the pub opened. They listened to some

Gilbert and Sullivan music on the stereo player. Lucy didn't care for Gilbert and Sullivan, she found it too stilted and flowery, but it was Mrs Hobden's favourite music.

At last the time came for them to go down the road for a drink.

"What do you think of my mother?" asked Brian as they sat under the oak beams in the pub.

"Well, she…" Lucy wondered what to say. "She's alright."

"She's been a widow a long time – my father died in the war."

"Oh. Do you remember him?"

"No, he died just before I was born."

Brian and his mother seemed so ultra-respectable that Lucy suddenly wondered if he was really illegitimate. She smiled as she imagined the horror on his face if she should suggest it, then hastily composed her face before he could catch her smile.

Afterwards they walked up the meadow path again. The buttercups were now tightly closed, and a chill mist rose from the grass.

"Would you like a bit of moral support?" asked Brian, putting his arm around Lucy's waist. Instinctively she pushed his arm away, then wished she hadn't; it seemed so silly to object.

"Don't you like an arm around your waist?" he asked in an injured tone.

"That depends whose it is," she answered.

They walked on in silence, broken only by the squeak of Brian's shoes and a cuckoo calling in a chestnut tree.

"Did I embarrass you by putting my arm around your waist?" persisted Brian.

"For goodness' sake, don't hold a post-mortem on it!" said Lucy irritably, knowing it would be useless to try to explain. Why couldn't men understand that a girl needs to be emotionally involved before getting physical? Why do they try to rush things? "I'd like to go home now, please," she said tiredly. "It's getting late."

"Would you like to see that film at the Odeon?" asked Brian as they drove back to Redfold.

"It's a war film, isn't it?" said Lucy doubtfully.

"Yes."

"Oh, I don't like those," she replied, relieved.

He stopped the car in Light Street, suggesting, "I'll drop you a line about future events."

"No, don't bother." Lucy tried to make her voice gentle. "It won't work out, you know, we're too different. Goodbye." She got out and shut the car door quickly, running up Crimmond's steps. Up in her attic, she sat on her bed drinking weak coffee, frowning at the roses on the wall. Why couldn't she find a man she could really fall for, like Mr Roberts? She wouldn't push *his* arm away! Why wouldn't such a man want her?

She knew why really: she had nothing much to offer. She was physically attractive, but that wasn't enough. She was too insular, too interested in herself and not in other people. She knew she didn't have much love in her to give anyone, except, perhaps, if she had a child... but that would only be because a child would be an extension of herself.

She went to bed and lay looking up through the skylight

window. The sky was soft as dark blue suede, speckled with little milky stars. Maybe she could write a poem about it; life seemed less futile when she was writing. A line came into her head. She reached for the bedside light, switched it on, and picked up the pencil and paper she kept on the bedside table. She scribbled a few words, switched off the light and let darkness flow back into the room. She felt calmer, and closed her eyes.

4
June

One Saturday morning in June Lucy stood looking out of her skylight window, watching swifts skimming across the slates. Their shrill, plaintive squeals echoed around the chimneys, and Lucy caught a whiff of honeysuckle from a garden far below. She wondered whether to go out for a walk or stay in and write her diary. Maybe she ought to give the flat a good clean. Last time Mrs Ashby, the landlady, had been up to collect the rent she'd glanced around the room with distaste and asked Lucy would she like to borrow the vacuum cleaner? She'd do it tomorrow… She was just about to pull her diary box out from under the bed, when there was a knock at the door.

"Lucy," called Ruth. "Are you in?"

"Hello." Lucy opened the door.

"Bill and I are going to a party tonight," announced Ruth. "Would you like to come this time?"

"Yes, please." Lucy was glad she didn't have to refuse again.

"Be ready by half past seven," Ruth told her.

Lucy wondered what to wear. Recently she'd bought a long ankle-length dress with big blue roses all over it but hadn't had an occasion to wear it to yet. She'd wear it tonight.

That evening, Bill drove them down to a seedy little terraced house in one of Redfold's back streets. There were cars parked all up the road, and loud pop music came pounding out of the front door. *Oh no*, thought Lucy, *it's going to be one of those parties where you're nearly deafened and can't hear anyone who speaks to you.*

There was a lot of drink, a lot of people and she didn't know any of them. She sat sipping cider in a corner, her eyes roaming over the shadowed faces around her. There was a lull in the music for a moment.

"You look lonely," said a voice beside her. "Can I get you anything?"

Lucy looked up. It was a youngish man with dark hair and quick hazel eyes. She felt a sudden predatory interest in him.

The loud music started up again. "I'm fed up with all this noise," she had to shout above the music.

"So am I!" he bawled back. "Let's go somewhere quiet." They went out into the hall, where he suggested, "Shall we go for a walk down by the river?"

"Yes, alright." She liked the slight huskiness in his voice.

"You're not out with your boyfriend tonight then," he

remarked as they strolled down to the end of the road. The song "In the Summertime" floated out behind them.

"I haven't got one," replied Lucy.

"That's what I was trying to find out."

"Yes, I know you were!"

"I can't think why you haven't got one," he continued. "You're very pretty."

"I don't go out much, really."

They came to the river, where foliage grew grey and mysterious in the twilight. They wandered past giant rhubarb leaves like green toadstools, and hemlock that exuded a heavy aromatic smell, their white floury blossoms tickling Lucy's arms.

"What's your name?" he asked.

"Lucy."

"I like that, it suits you, there something little-girlish about you. My name's Joe… May I ask you an impertinent question?"

"What is it?"

"How old are you?"

"Guess," she couldn't resist replying.

"Twenty?"

"No."

"I don't know whether to go up or down." He laughed. "Nineteen or twenty-one?"

"Twenty-three."

"Really? You don't look it."

"I don't feel it."

"I'm thirty-three, but I don't feel it either." He put his arm around her and tried to draw her to him. She didn't want him to kiss her yet; it would spoil things if they rushed too much at first.

"No?" His voice was quizzical.

"No."

"Why not?"

"I don't know you well enough to want to."

"Fair enough." He dropped his arm from her. She liked the way he took her at her word, without any stupid remark about her being shy. Yes, she liked it very much.

"Where do you come from, Lucy?" asked Joe.

"Cornwall," she replied. "From a little town called Carnmisk."

"Do you? Yes, I thought you weren't from around here. I'm from Somerset myself, near Yeovil." That explained a certain pleasant burr in his speech. Sometimes Lucy was proud of her Cornish origin, and sometimes she was ashamed of it, according to who she was with. She felt a sense of comradeship with this man, also from the West Country.

"What made you leave Cornwall to come here?" he asked.

"I wanted to leave home," she answered. "I felt I was living a too secluded life. My father didn't want me to leave, though."

"Are you very fond of him?"

"Yes, I suppose so."

"Can I tell you something?" he continued, as they wandered across damp grey grass. "Without being sloppy, if your father thinks you're the sweetest girl in the world, then he's dead right."

Lucy didn't like that; it was too sentimental. It was no good saying it wasn't sloppy, because it was.

"You're the second sweetest person I know," he told her.

"Who's the first?" she asked, as she thought he meant her to.

"I can't tell you," he replied.

Hmph, thought Lucy cynically, *I suppose he wants me to think he's got a broken heart or something.* She felt suddenly chill in her thin cotton dress. "Let's go back," she said. "I'm cold."

"Okay," he agreed.

The moon beamed softly yellow as they walked back up the dark street.

"There aren't many really pretty girls about," remarked Joe, "though there're a lot who try to be. But when I saw you tonight I thought, *There's a pretty girl...* Shall I drive you home?"

"Yes, I don't want to go back to that party. I'll just tell my friend I'm going."

Lucy looked around a long time before she found Ruth with Bill in the back garden. She felt awkward at disturbing them but managed to tell Ruth rather breathlessly that she'd had enough and was going home.

Joe was waiting for her in the road outside. "This is a busted old car, really," he apologised, opening the door of a dilapidated old black Ford.

"I don't mind." Lucy climbed into the uneven seat. "I don't like blokes with flashy cars." She managed to direct him back to Light Street, where they jerked to a stop.

"When will I see you again?" asked Joe.

"When do you want to?"

"Can you meet me on Monday night and go for a drive somewhere?" he suggested.

"Alright," she agreed.

They arranged that he'd wait for her at eight o'clock at the bottom of Light Street.

"You will be there, won't you?" he asked anxiously.

"Of course I will," she replied. "Why shouldn't I be?"

"I dunno… some girls let you down, but you wouldn't. Goodnight, Lucy."

He didn't try to kiss her, just sat and lit a cigarette. Lucy suddenly thought how sexy he looked lighting his cigarette, his hair in a little drake's tail over his collar.

"Goodnight." She realised she'd better not sit there looking at him, or he'd think she was waiting for him to kiss her. "See you Monday." She ran upstairs to her attic in elation and sat on her bed thinking for a long time.

*

Next morning Lucy woke up to a wet Sunday, so she decided to stay in and clean the flat. Then she remembered that Ruth had the vacuum cleaner. *Damn!* thought Lucy. *I can't go and disturb her now; she'll be sleeping off last night and she's probably got Bill in there too.*

Lucy's thoughts turned to Joe, the man she'd met last night. She wondered if she'd end up in bed with him, or even marrying him. No, she didn't think she'd want to marry him; he was too sentimental. He'd irritate her after a while. But she liked him and would probably feel attracted to him when she knew him better. She wondered what his job was. He wasn't "bingo", but something in the way he spoke told her he wasn't of the professional class either. After breakfast, she started to write about him in her diary.

*

The June weather turned wet, and rain fell in grey lines as Lucy walked down Light Street on Monday evening to meet Joe. There was his black car at the bottom of the hill, gleaming wet. She felt excited as she swished the drops off her umbrella and climbed in beside him.

"Dead on time," he remarked. "Where shall we go?"

"Where do you think? It's too wet for the river."

"Let's drive around for a bit."

The car swished through the rain, and Joe suggested, "Let's go and sit in the car park for a while. It's not very romantic, but we'll be dry."

They drove to the car park behind Sainsbury's. Joe jerked the car to a stop, then sat looking at Lucy, observing, "It seems such a long time since I last saw you, more like two weeks than two days." He touched her hair. "I like your hair… I'm sorry, that sounds like a cliché, but it isn't meant to be. You remember I wanted to kiss you last time?"

"Yes."

"Well, do I know you well enough now?"

"Well… if you like."

He put his hand under her chin and tilted her face upwards. Then he laid his lips on hers, sending electric shock waves of desire coursing through her body… Rain hammered on the car roof, and Lucy found herself thinking how grown-up it was to be locked in a man's arms, kissing. It was rather an incongruous thought, since she was supposed to have been grown-up for years.

"Have you had many boyfriends?" asked Joe curiously.

"No," she replied, "I've been out with blokes sometimes, but I've never had a steady boyfriend."

"Either there's something wrong with the male population, or you've kept yourself hidden away."

"I suppose I led a secluded life at home, until I suddenly realised I was twenty and had never been out with a boy, so I started going out dancing and joined lots of clubs, but nothing came of it."

"Am I the first man to kiss you?"

"No, I went out with a bloke a couple of years ago, and I let him kiss me just to see what it's like. But I didn't like it at all – he opened his mouth and slobbered all over mine; it was horrible. I don't see the point of kissing anyone unless I like them."

"You let me kiss you."

"Yes… because I like you."

"I take that as a great compliment, Lucy."

He kissed her again, his hands wandering over her breasts. She liked that but pushed his hand away when it crept up her legs; she felt shy of him doing that.

"Well, you can't blame me for trying." He laughed. "What's the time?"

"Why?" She was annoyed at him worrying about the time so early. "It's only half past eight."

"Look here." He frowned. "I don't want to hurt you."

"How could you?"

"There's something I must tell you… I'm married."

"Oh." She was surprised, and disappointed. But she didn't want him to think he mattered a lot to her, so she said lightly, "It doesn't matter."

"Doesn't it? I thought it would. I'd better take you home now, I told my wife I was just going out to get some petrol."

Lucy felt rather flat as they drove back; she'd expected to be out with Joe all evening. He stopped outside Crimmond and asked, "Do you want to see me again, or shall we call the whole thing off?"

"No, don't call it off. I'd like to see you again if you can manage it."

"Right. Thursday evening, eight o'clock, usual place. Okay?"

"Yes." Lucy smiled, and climbed out into the rain.

Up in her attic she sat drinking milky coffee, rain drumming on the skylight above her. She liked Joe; there was something endearingly old-fashioned and almost boyish about him. She felt at ease with him, so she was able to be her natural self with him. It was such a pleasure to find someone she could be natural with. He wasn't Luke Finn or Mr Roberts, but he was just… nice. She pushed away a little niggle of guilt at the thought of agreeing with him to deceive his wife, by arranging to see him again. *Well, he started it*, she justified to herself. *He kissed me and "lit the fire" before he told me he's married.*

*

Thursday evening came around, wet again.

"We've got about half an hour," said Joe as Lucy got into the car. "I've left the washing in the launderette, I'll go back and get it afterwards."

They drove to a bit of deserted wasteland, screened by bushes, at the top of Light Street.

"You could have come up to my flat," suggested Lucy.

"Could I?" He sounded surprised. "I didn't think you'd like it. We will next time… You could blackmail me, you know."

"Well, I won't. I don't even know your full name."

"Joseph Broome."

"Would your wife be upset if she knew about me?"

"Yes, she would."

"And you don't want to upset her?"

"God, no." He lit a cigarette and offered her one.

"No, thanks, I don't smoke. How long have you been married?"

"Five years."

"How old is she?"

"Thirty-three, same as me."

"Have you got any children?"

"A little boy, Roland, he's two years old. I'd rather drown with a millstone round my neck than have anything happen to him."

It had stopped raining, and the clouds peeled back in a watery pink sunset. Joe took a draw on his cigarette, and asked, "Can you understand that I could go to bed with you and still love my wife?"

"Yes… sex and love are different, I suppose."

"My wife's perfect for me in every way, except that she doesn't want sex as often as I do. I get so frustrated, so bloody frustrated." He took another puff, blew out the smoke and admitted, "To put it bluntly, I want you for sex."

"I wouldn't like being the 'other woman' in a triangle," said Lucy slowly, "but I might as well admit that I find you attractive."

"Can I ask you a very personal question?"

"What is it?"

"Have you ever been to bed with anyone?"

Lucy hesitated, then she whispered, "No, I haven't."

"It's a good thing to be a virgin."

"I'm rather ashamed of it, really."

"I can soon alter that! It would be easy to fall in love with you, Lucy... Why don't you find a nice single bloke?"

"How?" Lucy's voice was bitter. "They're not interested in me; I'm too reserved and awkward."

"That's what attracted me to you, as well as your face. The more I see you the more attracted to you I am, everything about you and the way you think."

"You know," she said thoughtfully, "you being married makes things easier, in a way. With a single bloke I'd feel we'd be sizing each other up as a potential husband or wife, so it'd make us awkward with each other. But I don't feel I've got to try and impress you, so I feel at ease with you."

"Good, I feel at ease with you too. Well, do you want to have an affair with me?"

"Well," Lucy was longing for him to kiss her again, "let's see how it goes."

She leant back blissfully as he kissed her, his hands roaming over her breasts.

"I'd like to get at those," he murmured, feeling her dress at her throat. "There should be a zip there."

Lucy was annoyed. Didn't he have the sense to realise that most dresses have zips at the back, or did she have to tell him? Eventually her desire overcome her modesty, so she whispered, "There's one at the back."

She sat acquiescent as Joe unzipped her dress and gently pulled down her clothes to reveal her bare white breasts.

"What beautiful breasts!" he exclaimed, caressing them. "They're like two warm white loaves." He kissed them all over, then muttered, "I'd like to undress you, to peel off each layer—"

She pushed his hand away from up her legs, then asked, "What are you laughing at?"

"The way your hand couldn't move fast enough to push mine away! Why is that forbidden?"

"Because it is," said Lucy shortly, not wanting to tell him it was the wrong time of the month.

They kissed again, and Lucy remarked, "Do you know what my mother said when I left home? She said don't go out with any married men!" She laughed ruefully, then gave a little shiver as she remembered the worried look on her mother's face. Shaking off the moment's unease, she smiled as she lay on Joe's shoulder with his arms around her. "Do you know what I like best about you? Your voice – it's lovely and husky."

"I've never been told that before." He laughed. "I'm

scared to speak now!" He suddenly jerked up and asked, "What's the time?"

"Nine o'clock."

"Hell, the washing must have been done ages ago. I must go back now."

He dropped her at Crimmond on the way down, and they arranged to meet at her flat on Saturday. "Ring the bell for flat number 6," she told him as she climbed out of the car.

Lucy sat up in her attic in the twilight, thinking. She wondered if she ought to feel ashamed of letting Joe go so far with her when she hadn't known him a week yet. *No*, she thought, *life's too short to be proud or shy just for the sake of it. I like him, I'm attracted to him, I won't be young for ever, so I'll take this chance while it's offered.* She knew she'd go to bed with him when he asked her, and she knew she was making do with second best. She knew that if she'd met Joe a few years ago she wouldn't have slept with him, because she'd have hoped to find a better man than him sometime. Not that twenty-three was old, but if she'd never had a steady boyfriend by twenty-three, then it was obvious she didn't have what it takes to get one. So she'd take what was offered to her – Joe. Again there came that little niggle of guilt that he wasn't hers to take...

She thought of her parents, how horrified they'd be at her behaviour if they knew. *But Mum married young*, Lucy argued to herself, *she doesn't know what it's like to go on through your twenties without ever having had a man, driving yourself mad thinking what you're missing and wondering what it's like.*

She remembered vague hints and warnings her mother had given her about men, over the years. *The trouble with Mum*, thought Lucy resentfully, *is that she regards men as either dangerous or desirable – they either want to seduce you or marry you, so you run away from one kind and run after the other. She can't see them just as people with whom you can be friends, such as men you meet at work, and neither can I...*

It started to rain again, in little flurries that pattered on the skylight. Lucy switched on the light and got ready for bed.

*

She lived in a dream until Saturday, when the weather cleared and June sunshine beamed into her attic again. She spent the morning cleaning and tidying the flat, then went out in the afternoon for the weekend food shopping. It seemed that colours everywhere were sharper and brighter after the week's rain. Grass in the churchyard glowed vivid green, and flowers in the street market seemed to shout gloriously at her.

She couldn't settle to doing anything in the evening, so she curled up on her bed with her book of folk songs, waiting for the doorbell to ring. Eight o'clock came, then the minutes dragged on to five past. *Oh no*, she thought desperately, *maybe he couldn't get away tonight.* A sudden peal at the bell jerked her up. She flew to the door and ran downstairs.

When she opened the door to Joe, Lucy saw him as if meeting him for the first time again. She noticed the way his dark hair grew to a peak on his forehead, and the slight stoop of his shoulders in his brown tweed jacket. Laughter lurked in his hazel eyes as he looked at her, and she felt suddenly shy of him.

"Come up and see my attic flat." She turned abruptly, and he followed her upstairs. It seemed odd to see him standing in her room, the scene of so many private thoughts and deeds. He shut the door behind him and clasped her in his arms. They kissed, and his hands ran all over her body, setting off those electric shocks of desire again.

"How did you manage to get away tonight?" asked Lucy.

"You think I'm chained or something?" asked Joe quizzically, as he sat down in the chair and pulled her onto his knee.

"Well," she remarked, feeling deliciously confused, "I hope you haven't left any washing in the launderette this time."

"No," he replied, unzipping her dress, "I told my wife I was going to see Alf, that's my friend who had the party where I met you. My wife didn't come then because we didn't have a babysitter. I do go and see him sometimes, so she didn't think it odd tonight… Is that nice?" he asked softly, fondling her bare breasts. She said nothing, and he laughed.

"What are you laughing at?" she asked.

"The way you don't answer! They're a gorgeous pair… am I the first man to handle your breasts?"

"Yes."

"I take that as a great compliment."

"You needn't," she began, then decided to let him take it so if it pleased him.

"All this is new to you, then," he said almost reverently. "Tell me – why do you let me?"

"Because I like you."

"You've got a lovely body, Lucy. It's time a man handled you, or one day you'll grow old and wish a man had had you."

More kisses, then Joe asked, "Haven't you ever thought it would be nice to have a naked man in bed with you?"

"Sometimes…"

He laughed and kissed her again, muttering, "I'd like to do things to you."

"What things?"

"Well, for a start I'd like to lay you on that bed and gently take your virginity from you. Would you like that?"

"I don't know," whispered Lucy, hiding her face in his tweed jacket. "Would it spoil my chances of getting married one day?"

"Of course not. My wife wasn't a virgin when I married her, and I'd been with other girls before."

"How many?"

"I don't keep count! Promise me something, Lucy: when you get married, marry someone who likes poetry and music, and realises you're a person with feelings. Some men haven't got any finesse; they go too roughly the first time with a girl, hurting her so she's apprehensive next time. But that won't happen to you – some unseen power's taken you to me."

June

Lucy stifled a desire to laugh, and observed, "I don't want to get landed with a baby."

"I don't want to land you with one either! But I won't let that happen."

"How not?"

"Well, when was your last period?"

Lucy was embarrassed at his mention of that essentially female subject, yet also it seemed to enhance their intimacy. "I've got one now," she whispered.

"Let me know when it's finished," he said, playing with her hair, "then that'll be a safe time… I should be going back soon." The room had dimmed to grey.

"Don't go yet." Lucy nestled her head on his shoulder. "I wanted to ask you, where do you live?"

He hesitated, then muttered, "On Pains Road, the other side of the railway. Why do you want to know?"

"I just wondered. What's your job?"

"I work for the corporation, delivering things in vans."

"Oh." She was disappointed at such a humdrum job but felt a new respect for him when he told her, "I also get paid a bit for playing the piano in pubs."

"Do you? I'd like to hear you."

"Come and hear me next Friday if you like, at the Rat's Castle. Are you musical?"

"A bit, but I like to think I'm literary. Would you like to read some of my stories?"

"Yes, very much."

Lucy got up and stuffed some stories in a big envelope for him, and he asked curiously, "Don't you get lonely up here in your bedsitter?"

"Yes, sometimes. That's why I don't want you to go back yet."

"I thought it was because of *me* that you didn't want me to go." Joe laughed ruefully. "Ego! You know, Lucy, even if you hadn't told me you're a virgin, I'd have known. It's obvious you've had no sexual experience at all. There aren't many virgins about."

"Oh. Am I rare then?"

"You're a very rare and unusual girl, and if I wasn't already married I think I'd get around to asking you. You're just the sort of girl I go for; I feel protective towards you. You know what? You're too good for this world."

"Don't be ridiculous. I'm very human."

"You're too good for me, anyway."

They kissed again, and Joe whispered, "I really must go now. What day would be okay for me to come next week?"

Lucy paused to think. "Tuesday," she replied.

"Will that be alright?"

"Yes." She knew what he was asking her.

She sat for a while in the dusk after he'd gone. She knew, as sure as the sun would rise next morning, that she'd lose her virginity at last on Tuesday evening. A distant diesel train went grinding through the station, and the stars winked at her through the skylight.

5
Midsummer

There was a thunderstorm on Monday night. Lucy woke up with a start at the sound of rain pounding on the skylight. A lurid flash lit up the room for an instant, followed by a crash of thunder. Lucy dreaded thunderstorms; the sinister growl of thunder frightened her, ever since she was a child. She'd hoped she'd outgrow many things on becoming an adult, but all her fears and failings seemed to get worse as she grew older.

She switched on the bedside light and tried to read, but kept waiting for the light to flicker, then for the thunder. A ridiculous thought crossed her mind – maybe she'd be struck by lightning and have to die still burdened with her virginity, when she was just a day away from losing it!

The storm died away at last, and Lucy slept uneasily until morning. Looking up out of the skylight, she saw the sky swept all clean and bright, like a bird's blue egg, and the slates gleamed silver in the sunlight. As she walked to work along by the golf course, she beheld it as if for the last time, for she'd be different when next she saw it. The turf rolled smooth and green, spotted with wet buttercups.

When she left work at five o'clock that afternoon, Lucy felt she wanted to say goodbye to everyone, as she wouldn't be the same tomorrow. Up in her attic she got her tea ready, trying to quell the nervous waves that churned inside her.

"Oh hell!" She rushed out to the toilet. "I wish I didn't get diarrhoea whenever I'm nervous!"

She decided to have a bath before Joe came. She rattled at the bathroom door. It was bolted.

"Who's that?" called Ruth from inside.

"It's me – Lucy. I was going to have a bath."

"You'll have to wait." Ruth's voice echoed from the basin. "I'm washing my hair."

Lucy retreated to her room and tried to read. Ten minutes later Ruth banged on the door and called, "I've finished. Funny time for you to have a bath, isn't it? You usually have it later."

"Yes," stammered Lucy, "I feel tired tonight, I'm going to bed now."

"Oh. Well, I'm going out, so I won't disturb you. Goodnight."

Lucy was relieved to hear Ruth go out at half past seven, as Joe wasn't due until eight o'clock.

He came.

"I've read your stories." He handed them to her. "I like

them very much. They're warm and human; they pulsate from page to page."

Lucy was pleased but didn't attach much literary value to his praise. She put the stories away, then stood there, waiting for him to kiss her.

"You deserve something better than this situation," observed Joe, putting his arms around her.

"I can't get it," she replied sadly. "It's better to have a little of something than none at all. You know the old proverb: half a loaf is better than no bread!"

"You're very wise. But I've got my cake and eating it, so to speak." He kissed her, and murmured, "You don't want to stay a virgin for ever, do you?"

"No, I've been wanting to get rid of it for years!"

"Shall we get into bed?"

"Alright then." Lucy suddenly felt rather business-like about it. She felt shy as he undressed her but felt a bit ridiculous when they both stood naked. It seemed like being a couple of monkeys, somehow. *Well, this is it*, she thought as they got into bed.

She found it an odd experience, very painful and very undignified.

"Relax, relax," whispered Joe. "It's alright, I won't hurt you." But it did hurt, though not so badly after a while. *It's like being constipated in reverse*, she found herself thinking ludicrously. It all seemed slightly comic, the writhing and heavy breathing…

"That was lovely, Lucy," sighed Joe when he'd finished. "Did you enjoy it?"

"No, I feel all sore and bruised inside."

"You're not upset, are you?"

"No." Indeed, she felt flat and empty of emotion.

They lay squashed together in the single bed, and he stroked her hair as she buried her head on his shoulder. She liked the feeling of security his gentleness gave her; she craved for love, even a counterfeit one like this.

"I like this better than sex," she remarked.

"You'll like sex when you get used to it." He laughed. "There's nothing like it, I could do it all day and night and just stop for meals!"

"Is it better than writing stories?"

"Oh yes, better than anything! You did very well tonight; you didn't scream and want to stop, and I think more of you. I think more of you each time I see you – sometimes I think more about you than my wife."

"Her name's Rosemary, isn't it?"

Joe stiffened, and asked quickly, "How did you know that?"

"I looked you up in the voters' list in the library."

"You did, did you? You're a little detective, aren't you!"

"What did you tell her tonight?"

"I said I was taking the car to be repaired, which means I ought to go soon. You don't mind, do you?"

"Yes, of course I do! But I don't want to get you into trouble. Go on then."

Lucy tried not to laugh as they got dressed. It seemed such an anti-climax, fumbling with bra straps and knickers, and Joe looked so comical in his vest and pants; it seemed somehow to de-sex him. *How important clothes are*, she reflected, *not just for warmth and modesty, but for identity as well.*

He kissed her, and asked, "Shall we try it again sometime?"

"I don't know... I associate it with pain now."

"No, don't think that, Lucy, it's the most enjoyable thing in the world. I'll come again on Thursday. Okay?"

"Yes, alright."

"Look after yourself until Thursday," he said tenderly, giving her a long, hard kiss before he went.

Lucy climbed up to look out of the skylight at the blue summer night. Chimneys and television aerials stood stark in the starlight, and an owl hooted somewhere. She felt calm and at peace with the world. It hadn't been a wonderful experience with Joe, but neither had it been a sordid one. It had just been rather pathetic. But at last she'd satisfied the curiosity and feeling of inferiority that had nagged at her for years. She knew as much as any woman now.

She wondered why she was able to be so natural and at ease with Joe. *I know why it is*, she decided. *It's because we've been honest with each other, right from the start, about what we want from each other.* She had no illusions about him or her feelings for him. He was the first man she'd met whom she'd found attractive and who also found her attractive, and they'd been able to let each other know. She felt rather sorry for him, though she didn't know why. Then came that niggle of guilt again, that she'd taken something that didn't belong to her... She shook it off, closed the window and went to bed. It was a calm night, and she slept long and deeply.

*

The roses on the wallpaper glowed richly pink in the sunshine next morning. They seemed to smile at Lucy, as if they'd witnessed last night's scene and shared her happiness. She felt very happy this morning, full of new knowledge and confidence. She felt she wanted to tell everyone she was no longer a virgin, to open the skylight and shout it from the chimneys.

It seemed odd that no-one at work noticed any difference in her, but things went on just as usual. Her new confidence even enabled her to be calm with Mr Roberts when he came in. She wondered what he'd think if he knew about last night. She couldn't have him herself, but she'd like him to know that another man had had her. But she just sat demurely as usual over her typewriter, and no-one guessed the exuberance within her.

She went for a long, slow walk in the lunch hour, seeing everything with new eyes. The thick oak trees and hawthorn bushes seemed to have acquired a new depth, and distant elms draped dark green and sad, somehow. Lucy felt a compassion for women in general, wondering if they all suffered such physical pain in losing their virginity. She wondered how it had been for her mother. She hoped it wouldn't be so bad on Thursday.

*

Thursday evening came, and Joe. She didn't feel shy with him anymore; their relationship had progressed beyond that now.

After the usual preliminary kisses, Lucy said, "Seeing

as you're always asking me personal questions, can I ask you one?"

"What is it?"

"When did you last have sex with your wife?"

"A long time ago, over a week ago."

"Is that a long time?"

"It is for me! Why do you ask?"

"Because I don't like the thought of you going straight from her to me."

He seemed amused at that, and laughed. "You're very human."

Then they undressed and got into bed. Lucy cried out in pain again, and Joe remarked, "Maybe I'm too big for you; maybe you should find a bloke with a smaller one." He said this quite seriously, and Lucy realised that his sense of humour was lacking in some ways. It made her feel suddenly lonely, that they could never fully understand and communicate with each other. How little they really knew each other, even though they were in bed together.

She was glad when it was over, and they lay quietly together.

"Doesn't it worry you that I might make you pregnant?" asked Joe, playing with her breasts.

"No," replied Lucy, "I trust you that you won't. But I'd rather have a baby by you than never marry and never have one."

"You must want a child very much." He kissed her nipples, saying tenderly. "You'll be suckling a baby there one day."

"Maybe."

"I could almost say I love you, Lucy. A man can love two women, I suppose… My wife would never sleep with me again if she knew about you."

This made Lucy feel uncomfortable, with that conviction again that she was taking something that didn't belong to her. She asked, "Do you believe in God?"

"Yes, I do."

"Do you feel guilty because of me? Do you think what we're doing is wrong?"

"It's wrong," he admitted, "but God's loving, so He'll forgive us."

"Not if we know it's wrong and carry on doing it," she was annoyed at his complacency, "though no-one's being hurt because of us, as long as your wife doesn't know. I'm much happier since I've known you."

"It pleases me very much to hear you say that. I do like your company, you know."

"Do you?" Lucy was pleased. "I like yours too; I feel at ease with you."

"I feel at ease with you too. You're becoming my mistress – we could go on like this for years."

"That wouldn't be much fun for me in the long run. I want to marry and have a family."

"You will, one day… Surely there must have been some man you've liked, in all this time?"

"Yes." She hesitated, then decided to tell him. "A couple of years ago I was in love with a man at work. Well, I thought I was, but I'm not sure since. I didn't feel sexually attracted to him like I do with you; I just felt so secure and happy in his company – everything was so *right* when I was with him. When I realised how I felt I went all shy with him and spoilt it all. Anyway, he married someone else in the end."

"Would you love him now?"

"I don't know. Maybe not. It doesn't hurt anymore when I think of him; it hasn't hurt for a long time now."

Joe glanced at the clock, then said, as she knew he would, "I ought to be going back now. She thinks I'm round at Alf's."

They got up and got dressed. "Wait," she said as he moved towards the door. "When are you playing the piano next?"

"Tomorrow, if it's Friday."

"Can I come and listen to you?"

"Well," he seemed unsure, "I'll be at the Rat's Castle up Neville Road behind the station. You'll have to go in by yourself; we can't risk anyone seeing us together. Be there at about quarter past eight."

*

A light rain fell as Lucy walked through the hot, tired streets on Friday evening. It splashed darkly on the dusty pavements, and Lucy breathed in the scent of wet gravel and roses in the gardens. The Rat's Castle was a sleazy little pub up the hilly street behind the station. Lucy climbed up past shuttered shops and warehouses in the orange evening light. The rain stopped, and the sun set red behind the signals, gleaming in the metal web of railway lines.

Music and the hum of voices floated out from the Rat's Castle's black brick walls. Lucy paused doubtfully outside the door marked "saloon", then went in resolutely. She groped through the smoky dimness to the bar, with her face averted from those around her. Was he there? Yes! There he was, sitting at a piano in a corner. He saw her, gave her a quick smile, then bent over the keys again.

Lucy bought a bitter lemon and retreated to a table near the piano, hoping – for once – that no man would approach her. She sipped her drink and listened. Joe was playing a ragtime blues tune, one of those melodies that is cheeky yet wistful. Lucy felt the yearning in its notes, and also the subtle nuance that used to mock her in such music; but now she laughed with it, for she knew all about it.

A light threw Joe's shadow on the wall, while Lucy watched his stooping shoulders, his little drake's tail of hair on his collar and his clear-cut profile. She had never admired him more, nor felt more attracted to him, than at this moment. It thrilled her to think that he was hers, that she could stroke that dark hair and lie on those shoulders. *No*, she checked herself, *he's not mine, he belongs to that woman called Rosemary who's borne his child and lives with him on Pains Road.*

Joe stopped playing, and Lucy raised her eyebrows at him in a mute request to speak. He frowned quickly and shook his head, then bent over the piano again. She sat dreamily listening for an hour, while the atmosphere thickened to a blue fug and spilt beer winked on tables in the dim light. Presently Joe got up, with a quick look at Lucy, and went outside. After a few minutes she followed him.

The air was fresh and clean outside the pub, and the sky gleamed pale green where the sun had set.

"Lucy!" Joe called from a doorway. "Go up to the field at the top of the road, and I'll meet you there."

Up there the cornfield lay soft and pale grey in the dusk. Lucy pressed against his dark figure as they kissed wildly, and Joe muttered in his husky voice, "I had to ask you to come. Seeing you sitting there when I couldn't touch you or talk to you made me want you like mad… Let's lie down here."

Lucy sank down deliciously in the damp, sweet-smelling corn, and found herself hungering for him. She discovered that she enjoyed sex; she wanted more, more, more of the hot, slippery, satisfying rhythm of it. A pale gold moon beamed down on them as they writhed in the corn, and Lucy breathed in the naked, erotic scent of the damp earth beneath them. The boom, boom, boom beat of the song "Look What They've Done to My Song, Ma" sounded faintly from the juke box of a distant pub.

It seemed too soon when Joe had finished, and Lucy asked, "Can we do it again?"

"I couldn't, not so soon. I'm satisfied."

"But I'm not," retorted Lucy almost petulantly. "I like it."

Joe laughed out loud. "She's discovered it and finds that she likes it! We'll do it again tomorrow."

They lay together in the sweet-scented dusk, and he remarked, "I was thinking when I came out tonight, and my wife was bathing little Roly – she doesn't deserve this, she's at home working while I'm here with you. I feel guilty; she's too good to treat like that. I was going to suggest calling the whole thing off with us, but it's easy to think you won't be tempted when you're not in reach of the tree."

"Would you have had an affair with anyone else if you hadn't met me?"

"No, I wasn't particularly looking for anyone. Why should I be? But when I first saw you I wanted to have you alone and make passionate love to you. When you wouldn't let me kiss you that first time I wanted you even more. But there's nothing special about me, you know."

"No, you're just a nice bloke."

"Why lose your virginity to me? Why not wait for marriage?"

"I might wait for ever."

"You're so pretty." He stroked her hair. "This situation isn't good enough for you, out in a cornfield with a married man."

"I won't be pretty for ever. I might as well make the most of it while I'm young."

"You're funny – you're reserved yet so modern in your attitude to sex."

"I enjoy it," she replied, pulling her dress over her bare thighs, "but I don't like you to see me."

"I know you don't! That's your modesty conflicting with your desire, and you combine the two very well. I like it with you – you ask for it and enjoy it without losing your dignity. My wife seems to think she'll lose her dignity by showing that she enjoys it. She never asks for it."

They lay silent for a while, with the corn darkening around them. Then Lucy asked, "You do like me as a person, don't you, not just for sex?"

"I like you very much," he reassured her. "I could get very emotionally involved with you… It's time we went back now."

But he just sat there looking at her, until she asked, "What are you thinking about?"

"I'm thinking how much I like you. You're a wonderful person, Lucy. I've never known anyone quite like you."

As they strolled back down the road above the railway, Lucy asked, "Did you learn to play the piano like that, or does it come naturally?"

"I can't read a note," he replied. "It just comes; something tells me where to put my fingers."

Lucy had great admiration for any artistic talent and felt an almost proprietary pride in him. A train went grinding along the line below them, and the signals winked green.

"I'm sorry I can't see you home," said Joe as they kissed by the brick wall of the station, "but I must go back home now. I'll come and see you tomorrow night, usual time. Okay?"

"Yes." Lucy smiled. "Goodnight, Joe."

She skipped through the dark, quiet streets in elation, and through the flower-scented park where bats almost brushed her face as they flitted past.

Back in her attic she remembered Joe's words about his wife. That feeling of guilt came back again, more of a pang than a niggle, this time. She didn't feel like a wicked adulteress or a scheming "other woman"; it had just seemed natural all along that she and Joe liked each other, so they went to bed together. His wife had seemed an unreal person to Lucy, just an inconvenience that meant Joe couldn't stay with her all night. But now she felt that conviction again that she was taking something that belonged to someone else – something that she didn't really value, but his wife did. She wondered if she ought to stop seeing him… no, she couldn't, not now that she'd discovered the wonderful experience of sex.

*

When Joe came next evening, Lucy announced half-heartedly, "I've been thinking."

"What about?"

"Us. Maybe we shouldn't see each other anymore."

"Why not?"

"Because you feel guilty about it, so do I and – as you say – your wife doesn't deserve it."

"No. I'd rather cut off my arms and legs than hurt her."

This made Lucy feel lonely. "I wish someone felt like that about me."

"It grows, that feeling," said Joe gently. "You know, if things were different, it could have been a big thing with you and me."

"We'd get on each other's nerves if we were married."

"You don't get on mine. I find you very compatible, and very interesting."

They kissed, and he laughed. "The way you kiss me now, anyone would think you're madly in love with me."

"I'm not."

"You like making love with me, though, don't you…? Alright, don't answer then!"

Forgetting their good resolutions, they undressed and got into bed. Lucy enjoyed it as much as the night before. "Why do you want two women at once?" she asked afterwards. "Just for variety?"

"I want *you*, as well as my wife," he replied, kissing her. "I need you."

"I like to feel needed; I suppose that's why I want children."

"You love children," he observed sentimentally.

"No, not other people's. But I want some of my own."

"You want me to make you pregnant?"

"No, not really. It would cause too many problems."

Joe suddenly remembered something. "Look here," he said excitedly. "Tomorrow my wife's taking Roly to visit her parents in Sussex for a week, so I'll be able to stay with you all night for all next week – no more creeping away at ten o'clock. Are you pleased?"

"Yes. Are you?"

"I feel guilty at being pleased that she's going away. I love her, you know. But I'm pleased that I'll be with you all night. I must go now, though."

"Where does she think you are tonight?"

"I told her I'd had an offer to play the piano in a pub this side of town. I'll come again tomorrow night, then, and stay with you 'til morning."

And so through all the last week of June, Joe came to Lucy every evening and stayed with her all night, leaving early for work in the mornings. Lucy discovered a lot during that week. She experienced the ecstasy of sexual orgasm, like falling over a cliff, only you know you're going to land safely. Now she knew why great orchestral pieces of music always come to a climax. She found what a warm, secure feeling it gave her to wake in the small hours and hear Joe's steady breathing beside her, and the patter of rain on the skylight.

And she discovered that he irritated her intensely. It was a combination of little things that annoyed her: the way he sang sentimental songs while he got dressed in the mornings, the way he made silly jokes and laughed at them, the way he left lather in the sink after he'd shaved... She was glad Ruth was away on holiday.

It seemed odd that life went on as usual at work, where no-one knew what was happening to her. Sometimes old Frankie, the messenger who brought the post round in the mornings, stopped to chat to her. He was a wizened little old man who was always grumbling. His sour little eyes followed one of the girl clerical assistants, and he grunted to Lucy, "Bloody miniskirts, exposing themselves like that. Still, you're not like that, Lucy, you're a good clean girl."

Lucy wished she had the nerve to retort, "How do you know whether I'm good or not? I was in bed with a married man last night, so fat lot you know about me!" But instead she just smirked and carried on typing.

On Friday evening she went to hear Joe play the piano at the Rat's Castle again. She sat in a dim brown alcove watching his shadow on the wall behind the piano, sipping bitter lemon and feeling happy.

During the evening a lady complimented Joe on his playing. Lucy listened as Joe boasted, "I've played in all sorts of places – pubs, parties, clubs, dances, everywhere. I've been playing since I was a kid."

He's like a little boy who's praised and laps it up, thought Lucy scornfully as Joe went burbling on. *Did I really let this garrulous bore seduce me? Yet I still want him.*

She was glad when their last night came. She liked sleeping with Joe, but she didn't like living with him. She was fed up with hearing him brush his teeth and spit in her sink every night, and fed up with his face across the table over her cornflakes every morning.

As they lay in bed early on Saturday morning, Lucy announced, "I'm going home for my summer holiday for two weeks."

"With your mum and dad?"

"Yes."

"I feel I'd like your parents," he remarked, "because they're reflected in you."

"You can't always go by that," replied Lucy cynically. "My dad hated his mother-in-law."

Joe sighed, and asked, "Don't you ever feel sentimental?"

"Yes, sometimes, but not in the same way as you."

"Can I write to you while you're away?"

"Yes, if you like. I'll give you the address."

They dressed, ate breakfast, then Joe asked, "When are you going away?"

"Tonight, on the sleeper train."

"Well, it's goodbye for a while, Lucy." He kissed her. "You're one of the sweetest people I've ever met. I'll always keep a place inside me for you."

"Do you think about me at work when you're driving along?"

"Yes, I often think of you and wonder how you are and what you're doing. Most women yap too much; it's rare and restful to find a nice quiet girl like you. I should have met you years ago. Goodbye, Lucy."

She wasn't sorry to see him walk out of the door but felt lonely when he'd gone. She made a mug of milky coffee and sat drinking it reflectively, watching sunlight patterns on the wall. Then she sighed, got up and started packing for her holiday.

6

July

That evening Lucy stood waiting on Paddington Station, eyeing the other female passengers and wondering with which one she'd have to share a sleeping berth. It turned out to be a dumpy grey woman who irritated Lucy by chattering non-stop and leaving her bedside light on half the night. Up in the top bunk, Lucy closed her eyes and ignored the stream of chatter, feeling excited as the mighty diesel train moved off, with heavy clankings and metallic grating noises.

She didn't sleep well; it grew so hot in the cramped compartment, and the woman snored in the bunk below. As Lucy tossed and turned she thought about Joe, wondering why she despised him a bit. *I know why it is,* she decided. *It's because he over-romanticises me; he doesn't see me as I really am. All that talk about me being so sweet and wonderful is a load of drivel, as he'd soon find out if he was married to me – and I know he'd have asked me to marry him if he was single.*

She slept a little towards dawn, and awoke to see greenish-white mist on fields, and clean little grey towns. The chill morning light was warmed with a pink haze from the rising sun, and daylight flooded into the compartment, making the close darkness of the past night seem unreal.

When the train arrived in Penzance, Lucy had a quick snack in the station café, then found the big green bus that went to Carnmisk. She loved these visits home, now that she wasn't tied to it anymore. She sat on the top deck and looked with fresh delight at the steep fields and valleys like puckered green velvet, where cows grazed. Her spirits rose even more when she saw the blue line of sea in the distance.

Carnmisk was a hilly little town, even steeper than Redfold. Lucy got off the bus and climbed up to the grey granite house in Palk Road where she'd lived most of her life. It wasn't a pretty house, but its walls were softened by honeysuckle that her father had planted when Lucy was a child. She climbed a flight of stone steps, opened the side gate and entered in at the green back door.

Her mother was in the kitchen. Whenever Lucy saw her after a long absence, she thought how almost young and pretty she looked, though she was in her late forties. Mrs Grey was tall and slim like her daughter, but her eyes and hair were darker. Lucy felt a calm affection for her mother and was pleased to see her.

Her feeling for her father wasn't calm. She had always either loved or hated him, according to her mood or age. They were too alike. Lucy saw her own faults and intolerances in him, though his were set even stronger in middle age. She'd often resolved she'd never end up like him but found herself growing more similar to him as she grew older.

Mr Grey worked at a printing works in Penzance. Lucy had never known exactly what he did there, as he hated his job so much that he never talked about it, becoming irritable if anyone dared to ask him about it. As a boy he'd dreamt of being an architect or even a playwright, but he'd left school in the 1930s depression, when there was widespread unemployment, so he had to take whatever job he could get.

He came in from mowing the steep back lawn. He was very pleased to see Lucy, his blue eyes beaming. He had intensely blue eyes, Lucy often wished she'd inherited them, undimmed with grey. She was proud of her father. He wasn't bald or fat or florid like many middle-aged men; he was lean and wiry, with those fierce blue eyes and a mane of grey hair.

They sat down for Sunday roast dinner in the comfortable brown dining room, and Dad grumbled, "The beaches are hideous with bingo people, Lucy, leaving litter all over the sand, guzzling chips and ice cream, blasting the air with radios. And you know Penmarth Meadow? Well, it's a caravan site now. The more I see of the world the more I agree with that quotation I read somewhere: 'I do not like the human race, I do not like its silly face!'" He poured more gravy on his cabbage, and asked, "Have you heard from Jim?"

"No," replied Lucy.

"Neither have we. We sent him a cheque for his birthday last week but haven't heard a cussed word from him."

"Maybe he's busy," suggested Lucy.

"Busy!" grunted her father. "What's he got to be busy about? Going to the pub?"

Dad felt great scorn for those he referred to as "pub people" and was disappointed that his son liked pub life. Lucy always stuck up for her brother when their father grumbled about him. This was not from any sense of duty but because she felt it looked sneaky and in bad taste for sister to run down brother to their father.

Secretly it pleased Lucy when her father criticised Jim. Jim was two years older than her and had achieved material success in his life. He was a chartered accountant, earned a large salary and lived in his own flat in Bristol. His success compared unfavourably with her lack of it, in her eyes. She was glad he wasn't married yet – that would be another success to chalk up on his slate. They had played together as children, but since then Lucy felt not the slightest affection for him. They were so different. Jim was interested in facts, figures and practical things, while she was interested in artistic and (she liked to think) intellectual things. She doubted if he'd ever read a novel in his life.

A high-pitched whine started up from next door's garden.

"Cussed row!" exploded Dad. "Old Pennick's got a new motor mower, Lucy. You never heard such a racket; it's worse than the beach!"

July

"They've put a funfair down by the beach now," observed Mum.

"Yes," spluttered Dad. "You never saw anything so vulgar! It's awful! The bingos are taking Cornwall over. It's like that quotation in the Bible, 'The meek shall inherit the earth.' I reckon that meant the common man taking over."

Lucy didn't agree but would have felt embarrassed expressing her religious beliefs to her father. He voiced his own opinions so strongly that she feared his scorn or disapproval if she should express any views contrary to his.

It started to rain after dinner, so they couldn't go out for a walk. They retired to the sitting room, where Dad opened the bureau, pulled out some papers and sat scribbling for the rest of the afternoon. Lucy knew that he was writing one of his long narrative poems. She hoped it wouldn't run to more than about sixty verses, as she typed out these poems for him, as a labour of love. She liked his poetry, but it was too rambling. He imagined himself back in the past, as an eighteenth-century tin miner or fisherman, and wrote about life and scenes as he pictured them, interwoven with a story. Lucy knew that her own desire to write was inherited from her father.

She eyed her parents curiously. It seemed odd that they sat there so quiet and calm, unaware of the change in their daughter. Yet how could they know she was no longer a virgin? She felt almost guilty keeping this knowledge to herself.

*

Next morning Lucy awoke to sunshine glowing pink through the curtains. It was Monday, so Dad had gone to work early. Lucy stretched, basking in the morning sunshine. It was good to be home again for a while.

She looked around the bedroom, at the flowered walls, white wardrobe and blue candlewick bedspread. It was the kind of room you could love, though Lucy didn't love it because she hadn't been happy there for the last couple of years before she left home. She remembered lying on her bed feeling lonely and resentful, that life was passing her by. If she hadn't known that romance and sex and marriage existed she'd have been quite content to jog along with her parents, writing stories and walking in the hills… but she'd known there was a sweet slice of life that she was missing, so she'd gone out to search for it. And had she found it? *No*, she thought sadly, *only a poor imitation*.

She wandered down to the beach in the morning. Her eyes were affronted by the new funfair her father had objected to so strongly. It really was an eyesore. All the holiday-makers were spread out like colourful ants on the sand. There were suntan-oiled women roasting in the sun, and dads being boisterous with beach balls. *How sexless men look in bathing trunks*, thought Lucy, *like Joe when he's got just his pants on.*

She turned away from the beach, up a steep lane hedged dusty pink with campions and valerian. It led up to the cliff path, where Lucy sat among sea-pinks on the turf and gazed out over the sea. It shimmered bright turquoise streaked with violet, and Lucy felt its peace flood into her soul…

July

After a walk along the cliff path, she wandered back home and sat shelling peas in the garden, singing quietly to herself a song she'd heard at the Railway folk club.

"That's a pretty song," observed her mother's voice behind her. "Where did you hear it?"

Lucy jumped. She hadn't realised that Mum was weeding in the flower border behind her. Too confused to think up a lie, she replied, "At a folk club."

"Oh." Mum's voice sounded doubtful. "Where is it held?"

"In a pub."

"Do you go there on your own?"

"Yes," answered Lucy defensively. "Why not?"

"You shouldn't really go to pubs on your own. Decent men don't think much of girls who frequent pubs, you know."

"But it's perfectly respectable," protested Lucy. "People go there to listen to music, not just to drink."

"Well, girls have to be careful," continued Mum. "There was a case in the newspaper the other day of a girl who was followed from a pub by a soldier, and he tried to seduce her."

Lucy felt like replying tartly, "Maybe that's what she went in there for!" But she just grunted and carried on shelling peas, irritated by her mother's attitude. She watched a blackbird hopping down the stone path through the rockery. Her father had built that rockery. The garden had been just a rough patch of heathland when Lucy was a child, but her father had produced beauty and order from its chaos. It had been hard work, but she knew he felt a deep satisfaction as he sat in the garden on summer evenings and surveyed his creation. He sometimes said that to leave a tiny portion of the world better than you found it, is the ultimate that most people can achieve in creativity.

She went for a long walk with her father that evening, up in the hills above Carnmisk. They didn't talk much as they walked, content to be silent together, each thinking their own thoughts. A rough stony path took them up through heathland, where rowan trees were in bloom, their big cream plates of blossom brushing their heads as they passed. Up on the high ground the turf was strewn with boulders, where Lucy and her father sat on a rocky ledge.

Dad rolled a cigarette and observed, "Well, Lucy, this is better than Surrey, isn't it?"

"Better to look at," agreed Lucy. She leaned back on a boulder and let all the beauty flow into her soul. *There's something melancholic in these long, olive-green summer evenings*, she reflected. *How tiny and far away the hedges look down there, like tufts of wool on green tweed… how deeply quiet it is here, not a sound but the cry of a curlew…*

"Well," remarked Dad at last. "It's time we were getting back."

There was a television programme later that Dad wanted to watch, featuring an Irish comedian who could often be very funny but also a bit blue at times. He made one dubious joke that Lucy found excruciatingly funny, but she stifled her laughter because her father wasn't amused. So great was her desire for his approval that she didn't dare laugh if he didn't, in case he thought her dirty-minded.

July

"He's not like he used to be," grumbled Dad when the programme was over. "He's gone dirty, like all of them now."

But if a joke is funny, puzzled Lucy to herself, *does it matter that it happens to be about sex? It's intolerant of Dad to dismiss all such humour as dirty.*

It rained during the night. Lucy liked to listen to it rustling at the window in the darkness. Early next morning she walked down to the beach before the holiday-makers invaded it. It was beautifully fresh after the night's rain. Ox-eye daisies lay like milk in the meadows, and the egg-brown sand stretched smooth and clean.

She took off her sandals and paddled along the shoreline, while the holiday-makers arrived and settled on their deckchairs and beach towels. Lucy kicked a plastic bottle under a rock. *No wonder Dad hates them*, she thought angrily, *leaving their rubbish around like that.*

Her father was home when she returned to the house in Palk Road; he had odd half days off sometimes. *What's he grumbling about now?* wondered Lucy, hearing his sardonic tones as she opened the back door.

"There's a women's lib female in the paper, Lucy," he looked up from a newspaper as she entered the kitchen, "who camped in a men-only club and refused to be moved, because she wanted women allowed in as members. I was just reading it out to Mum before you came in. Cussed women! They can't bear to think that men can be happy doing anything that doesn't include women. I don't want to butt in on Women's Institute meetings, so why should they want to invade men's clubs? I bet she's one of those aggressive types of women with more male genes than female. We'll all be hermaphrodites soon, with men getting more effeminate and women more mannish."

"I can't imagine people losing all interest in sex," observed Mum drily. "Not men, anyway."

Lucy was embarrassed at sex being mentioned in her parents' presence, but she was puzzled too. *Why did people believe this myth that men enjoyed and thought about sex more than women did? Mum's married, surely she knows that women like sex too? Maybe she doesn't...* Lucy shied away from the thought. It was so impossible to imagine her parents making love that it seemed almost indecent.

It rained for the next couple of days. The beach was deserted, where Lucy liked to wander along the wet sand watching waves crashing onto the rocks. She had often paced this beach in a deep depression a few years ago, feeling that no-one cared whether she existed or not. Her parents cared, of course, but only because she was their daughter, not because of who she was as a person. *But then*, she reflected, *I don't really love them. When you're a child you need your parents, but you don't love them. Then as you grow older you come to like or dislike them as people. I'm fond of them, but I wouldn't grieve terribly if I lost them. Anyway, why should anyone else care about me? I'm not a particularly loveable person.*

Wet grass licked her legs as she climbed up the path from the beach, past a field where a little black goat lurked. She wondered when the weather would clear.

*

July

It cleared on Saturday, when Lucy found a letter with a Redfold postmark on the hall mat. *It must be from Joe!* She grabbed it and ran up to her room, studying the writing on the envelope. It was a large flamboyant scrawl – rather immature, she thought, with gaps between the letters. She sat in her wicker chair and tore open the letter, scrawled in blue felt pen on large lined paper:

"Dear Lucy,

This is just a line to help you, should you be feeling lonely. I know what it's like to be alone. When I was a boy I suffered intolerably. I cannot, in this letter, explain. I was hurt for years. I went without, also for years. Every day was a struggle to exist, as it was for my mother, bringing up four of us after my father left us.

But you are young and very pretty, and do not want to read about some sad old story that lives within me. What lives within you, you think you've told me. But what about when you are married and have your dozen (?) children? What then, my lovely?

Would you like to know what really moves me? Can I tell you it is a simple buttercup, the hair on a bumblebee's leg, the powder on a butterfly's wing or the way a woman's chiffon scarf hangs across her shoulder...?

You may laugh, but if you do, 'tis in a kind fashion. Let's write about love, the greatest power on earth! Let's write about music, the power to petrify thousands in great concert halls. Let's write about man's dominant feature – his power to concentrate within steel shutter attention! There are none so blind as they who will not see. God give me eyes that see!

Have I lived, for a while, within these lines I've written?

God bless you,
Joe XXX"

Oh dear, thought Lucy, *what an awful letter! What a load of clichés and sentimental drivel! Poor Joe, I don't like to laugh at him, but really!*

The telephone rang downstairs. Lucy heard her mother talking to an old aunt. *Poor Dad.* She grinned to herself. *He'll have to endure a visit from them soon.* She went downstairs, where her father was sitting at the kitchen table after breakfast.

"That's Aunt Ethel, isn't it?" He looked up with a sour expression.

"Yes."

"I suppose they'll be coming here one Sunday soon," he grumbled. "I don't mind her so much, but I can't stand Uncle Harry. All he talks about is cussed football! He's got no imagination or opinions about anything. What's the point of them coming? They don't really want to see us, and I certainly don't want to see them. It's all so needless and empty."

Dad had no friends or social life; he didn't feel any need for it. Lucy wondered if he'd have felt the need for friends if he hadn't married. Probably not, with his negative attitude towards people in general. He often remarked, "People always let you down. The only people you can trust are your own family."

"But what about people who haven't got any family?" Lucy had argued. "It's hard for them to have no-one to trust."

"Yes, but life is hard," replied Dad, "and a lot of people won't face up to that fact."

Lucy didn't always agree with her father's cynical philosophy. She knew she'd absorbed many of his opinions when too young to question them, and sometimes felt resentful of his strong influence over her. He'd often unintentionally destroyed her confidence by his criticism. He'd have been most upset if he'd realised this, as Lucy knew he loved her very deeply, and only criticised because he worried about her, and wanted to direct her life in the way *he* thought was best. She'd had to get away from him.

They went out for a long walk together later, along a lane sunk in hedges where hogweed bloomed like balls of breadcrumbs and escallonia leaves exuded a sweet aromatic scent. *I'll miss all this when I go back to Redfold*, reflected Lucy, *but I need more than the countryside to fill my life.* They came to a clearing where yellow clouds of ragwort covered the turf and sat on a tufty hillock to eat their picnic.

"Those flying saucer-shaped clouds mean good weather's settled for a few days," observed Dad. "It's a pity you've got to go back next weekend. You're happy at Redfold, aren't you?"

"Yes, of course," replied Lucy brusquely. She didn't like him asking a direct question like that. A shiver of guilt ran through her as she thought of Joe, and of how horrified her father would be if he knew.

Joe didn't write any more letters during the following week, for which Lucy was grateful. On her last evening she sat alone up on the cliffs for a while. It was a quiet, still evening, with a sky like curdled milk and the mournful cries of seagulls echoing around the cliffs. Some words from a Bible Psalm came into her mind: "I will lift up mine eyes unto the hills…"

She was glad to be going back. She liked her parents' company, but two weeks of it was more than enough. Her father went with her on the bus to Penzance next day to see her off at the station. She wished he didn't look so sad and worried, almost as if he knew about Joe… though of course he didn't.

At last the train heaved and pulled out of the station. Lucy watched her father, tall and grey, waving to her with a half-smile on his face. She felt almost sad when the last glimpse of his grey head disappeared, but excited too. It had been a pleasant interlude at home, but she wanted to get back to real life at Redfold now.

7
Late Summer

Lucy's attic seemed to welcome her as she opened the door. Sunshine smiled through the skylight, and all her books, papers, pens, saucepans and everything seemed waiting for her to take them up and use them again. She made a mug of milky coffee. She had enjoyed her holiday, but it was pleasant to slip back into the routine of being independent again. A shiver of excitement shot through her as she wondered whether Joe would come today. Probably not, as he didn't know what time of day she'd be back.

She pottered about, unpacking and writing a bit in her diary, then ate some sandwiches she'd bought at the station. She climbed up on the chair to look out of the skylight. It was a beautiful high summer's day, with a blue haze on the distant hills. *Joe won't come today*, she told herself. *It's too good to stay indoors.*

She walked down along red-brick terraced streets to

the river. It was cool and green down there, with yellow waterlilies floating on smooth brown water, and coots clucking in the rushes. Lucy sat on the grass bank and watched a moorhen swim by with a family of furry chicks. Surrey wasn't as wildly beautiful as Cornwall, but it was pleasant and lovely in its own way.

As she idly watched some children paddling in the shallows, one of them caught her eye and smiled shyly. Lucy didn't usually notice children much, but this one was a pixie-faced little girl with eyes like bluebells, and Lucy thought how sweet she looked. The child ran back to her mother, who Lucy realised was Margaret Moore, a part-time clerical assistant at the Ministry. She'd been there about two months, only working in the mornings because she had young children at school. She was about thirty, with dark blue eyes and dusky hair. She'd tried to be friendly to Lucy at first, but Lucy had resented her because she felt jealous. She'd thought, *You've got a husband, children, a likeable personality – everything that I want. What do you want with me?* So she'd been churlish at Margaret's attempts to be friendly.

She wished now that she hadn't and wondered whether to make herself known. Yes, she would. She was lonely and needn't feel inferior to this woman anymore, since Joe. She stood up and walked past the group on the grass, saying, "Hello, Margaret."

"Hello, Lucy." Margaret looked up and smiled kindly. "Did you have a good holiday? Come and sit with us." She seemed to have forgotten the rebuff Lucy had given her at work, or to ignore it.

"Ken's away at work today," she continued as Lucy sat down on the grass. "He works on Sundays sometimes, so I thought I'd take the children out for a picnic by the river. Do you often come down here?"

"Yes," replied Lucy, "I like it here, it's lovely and quiet."

"Is that what you do on Sundays, just walk around by yourself?"

Lucy would have resented such a question from most people, but Margaret asked it in such a kindly tone – not nosey or pitying, just kindly – that Lucy didn't mind, and answered, "I like walking alone."

"What do you do when the weather's bad?"

"Potter around in my attic flat, reading or writing."

"What do you write?"

Lucy told Margaret about her stories and promised to let her read some. She hadn't felt so relaxed with anyone for years, except for her parents and Joe, in different ways. She thought how pleasant it was to be one of this little group by the river, instead of alone as usual. She felt that the children accepted her and didn't mind her being there. The two boys swam and splashed in the water. They had the same dark blue eyes as their mother and Sarah, the little girl.

"Would you like to come round for coffee and chat one evening?" suggested Margaret. "Ken works some evenings, so I'm alone then after the children have gone to bed."

"Yes, I would," said Lucy sincerely. She tried to calculate quickly when Joe was likely to come, then replied, "I'll come on Tuesday, if that's alright with you. I'll see you at work before then, anyway."

Back up Light Street, Lucy opened the front door of Crimmond and pounced on a piece of folded paper on the floor. She recognised Joe's scrawl immediately. He'd written: "*Dear Lucy, I called but you were out. I'll come tomorrow evening, usual time. JB.*"

So he'd come after all! Lucy almost kicked herself for going out. Well, she wouldn't have met up with Margaret then, and would have gone on being distant to her at work.

*

It was dreary going back to work next day. Trees by the golf course drooped dull green and tired as she walked past them; the freshness had gone from summer. Lucy felt depressed as she sat at her desk typing the usual correspondence about cattle farming and chicken manure.

It was the custom to bring back sweets for the Ministry staff after being away on holiday. Lucy had dutifully bought a tin of Cornish cream toffees for this purpose and dreaded having to go around the desks distributing them like a fairy godmother. Tea break came, so Lucy decided she'd better get it over with. The older women looked at her kindly as she approached them, while the girls regarded her with curious, cynical looks. Margaret gave her a conspiratorial grin, and Lucy felt that she had an ally among these people who seemed foreign to her at times.

"Have a Cornish toffee," she grunted, rattling the tin under Mrs Browning's nose.

"Thank you, Lucy, dear," gushed Mrs Browning. "Did you have a lovely time? What did you do?"

"Went for walks," muttered Lucy.

"Did you go swimming in the sea?" asked one of the girls.

"No, too cold." Lucy passed the tin along. At last they'd all had one, and Lucy retreated to her corner. *Thank goodness that's over*, she thought, then grimaced as she realised she'd have to repeat the same procedure at the afternoon tea break.

The first day back is always the worst, she reflected as she walked up Light Street after five o'clock. *I'll soon settle into it again.*

When eight o'clock came she waited anxiously for the doorbell to ring. Joe didn't come until half past. His face looked older, it seemed to Lucy, and his eyes less lively. He smiled tiredly, and asked, "Did you miss me?"

"Yes… a little bit."

"Oh. I missed you too… a little bit."

Lucy was disappointed. She'd have liked him to say he'd missed her sorely and longed for her return, though she knew that was unreasonable. She yielded blissfully to his kisses, hungry for him after a fortnight without him.

"I must ask you something," muttered Joe into her hair. "Has your period come yet?"

"No." Lucy had forgotten about it. "I suppose it was due about… last week."

"Are you sure?"

"It should have come by then, but it's not always regular. I suppose it's not a safe time for us now, is it, if it's due any day now?"

"It's not that I'm worried about. I'm scared I might have made you pregnant."

"Oh no, that's impossible." Indeed it did seem impossible that such a big thing could happen. "We kept within the safe time, didn't we?"

"I hope so, but we might have run over it. You'll let me know when your period comes, won't you?"

"Yes, of course I will."

Joe hesitated a moment, then he said awkwardly, "If everything's alright, and you're due any time now, then it means we can't go to bed just now."

Lucy was deeply disappointed. She'd forgotten the danger and had looked forward to being in bed with Joe. "Can't we use something?" she asked vaguely.

He laughed shortly. "I haven't got anything. My wife's on the pill."

Lucy was angry. He'd had a fortnight to prepare for making love safely with her, and he hadn't bothered.

"Are you very disappointed?" he asked in a low voice.

"No," lied Lucy, "I don't care."

"Yes, you do." He kissed her. "Look, I'll get something and come round on Friday. Okay?"

"Yes... but what about your piano playing?"

"I'll use that as an excuse to my wife. Are you on the phone here?"

"Yes, there's a communal one down in the hall. Why?"

"I'll phone during the week to ask if your period's come. I'm worried."

"I'm not." And it seemed odd to her that she wasn't. Was it because she refused to believe it could happen, or that she wouldn't mind if it did? She wasn't sure; she'd have to think about it.

"I hope you're right," muttered Joe. "I'll have to go now – she thinks I'm out getting petrol. What's your phone number?"

Lucy wrote it down on a scrap of paper. "Phone on Wednesday, if you must do it," she suggested. "That's halfway between now and Friday."

She pottered about aimlessly after he'd gone. She just couldn't grasp the fact that she might be pregnant. She tried to visualise all the problems – the shock and horror of her parents, the difficulties of bringing up a child alone, the freedom she would lose… But she just couldn't make herself feel worried or frightened; it was all so unreal. She vaguely thought it would be nice to have a child of her own; it would be something to live for. She'd once decided that if she wasn't married by the age of thirty she'd try to have a child anyway, before it was too late. That vow had been taken in her teens, when she hadn't seriously thought she'd ever carry it out, for of course she'd get married some time in her twenties. So far that seemed unlikely.

She didn't have the nerve to deliberately become pregnant by Joe, but if by chance it happened, then on the whole she'd welcome it. She might never get another chance.

*

Tuesday evening came, and Lucy went to visit Margaret Moore. Margaret lived in a red-brick terraced house in Blackdown Avenue, a long road that backed on to allotments behind the golf course. Lucy reached it through a maze of hilly streets and shrubby alleys heavily scented with privet blossom.

Margaret's blue front door opened directly on to the street. Lucy heard slow, laboured piano notes from the front window.

"Hello, Lucy," Margaret welcomed her. "I'm glad you've come. There's some cake left over from tea – we can finish it up with coffee when the children are in bed."

Lucy felt cosy and comfortable sitting in the back living room while Margaret worked through a pile of clothes to iron.

"I hate ironing," remarked Lucy. "Don't you find it dreary?"

"No, I don't mind it," replied Margaret. "I can think while I'm doing it."

"What about?"

"Oh, about people, about the children… all sorts of things. That's Paul doing his piano practice in his bedroom. We have to keep the piano in there, we've so little space here."

"I like this house," observed Lucy. "It's homely."

"Yes," agreed Margaret. "All houses have an atmosphere, and this house has a happy one. I like to think we've made it so."

"I expect you have – you seem a happy person."

"Yes, I suppose I am happy… There, that's enough for tonight." She folded the clothes away. "I must tell Paul to go to bed now; the others are already in bed."

She called him, and Paul came in. There was some good-natured argument between him and his mother about bedtime, and Lucy could see that they had an excellent relationship.

"Does your husband work late most evenings?" she asked as they sat over coffee and cake when Paul had gone to bed.

"Usually twice a week," answered Margaret, "and some weekends. He's a social worker in a remand home for boys with various problems."

"Does he like it there?"

"Yes, he's very fond of the boys, even the difficult ones." She told Lucy some of their case histories. Lucy knew that "problem children" existed, but she'd never thought much about it and was surprised at some of the things Margaret told her. She resolved that her child – if she had one – wouldn't end up a problem.

The doorbell rang, and a neighbour came in to borrow something. Lucy immediately labelled her as a "bingo woman", resenting her intrusion just when she and Margaret were chatting so easily together. When the woman had gone, Lucy asked curiously, "Do you like having her for a neighbour?"

"Yes, she's good-hearted and she amuses me," replied Margaret. "I couldn't talk to her about deep things or personal things, but she's alright to chat to superficially."

"But do you like talking superficially?"

"Yes, sometimes. It's a form of communication between people; they couldn't do without it."

"That's the trouble," Lucy confided. "People can't do without it, and I can't do it. That's why I sit in my corner at work and don't speak to anyone."

"But do you really want to speak to them?"

"I don't know... I suppose not," said Lucy thoughtfully, "because they only talk about superficial things. What's the point of talking just for the sake of it? It's so boring! I like being alone, but I get lonely sometimes... It's funny talking to you like this, but you're different; you're not like them. Why are you in that dreary job?"

"Because I'm not qualified to do anything more interesting. I met Ken when we were both in the sixth form at school. I hadn't thought I'd get married until my late twenties – there were so many things I wanted to do. I wanted to be a social worker or a hospital almoner. But then Ken happened, and we decided to marry after we'd done our A levels. I was going to go to university with him, but then Paul came along."

"Don't you ever feel bored at work?"

"No, not really, it's just a job to earn some extra money, and it won't be for ever. When the children are older I'll go to university and qualify in the same line as Ken, then we could work together. It's wonderful having children when you're young; I wouldn't miss it for all the interesting jobs in the world."

For a moment Lucy felt sad and cheated, then she thought with a warm thrill of the tiny new life that might be within her. She wanted to tell Margaret but decided it was too soon yet. She didn't know Margaret's moral opinions and principles; she might condemn Lucy for becoming pregnant by a married man.

"When will Ken be in?" asked Lucy, looking at her watch.

"Soon now," replied Margaret, glancing at the clock. "Would you like to meet him?"

"Not particularly." Lucy grinned. "You know I don't like meeting people."

"Well, I know now!" Margaret laughed. "Come again sometime. Ken's usually out working on Tuesday evenings."

"Oh, I nearly forgot." Lucy pulled a large, bulky envelope from her bag. "Here are my stories for you to read. That's if you want to?"

"Yes, I do," said Margaret sincerely. "I might not have time to finish them by next week, though."

"That's alright, keep them as long as you like. I'd better go now, see you at work tomorrow."

*

Just after Lucy had finished her tea on Wednesday evening, Ruth called outside the door. "Lucy, are you in? There's a man on the phone for you."

Lucy grimaced and ran downstairs.

"Lucy?" Joe's voice sounded cracked and husky. "Has it come yet?"

"No."

"Aren't you worried?"

"Well, there's nothing I can do but wait. Are you coming on Friday?"

"Yes."

"We can talk then; I don't like talking on the phone. Goodbye."

"But Lucy… alright, goodbye then."

*

Next evening, being Thursday, Lucy decided to go to the Railway folk club, where she hadn't been for a long time. It was a wet, steamy evening, very hot and beery in the club's room. There was a new group performing called the Thackers, consisting of two men and a girl. They sang in a wild, haunting way, the girl with her husky voice and sagebrush hair; the men with their bushy beards and violins. *There's something yearning and heart-rending about violin music*, thought Lucy. *It makes me think of the wild sea and cliffs at Carnmisk beach.* She felt she wanted to soar with them and cry with them in their music.

Then one of the men played a solo on a recorder. It was wild and pagan, like the pipes of Pan. Lucy listened almost mesmerised.

When it was over she skipped back through the wet streets where lamplight glimmered in the puddles, singing to herself, elated and free as the wind.

*

Friday came, and Joe. Lucy saw the worry in his eyes as she opened the front door.

"No, it still hasn't come," she told him as they climbed the stairs.

"I'm worried sick!" he burst out, when they were safely up in the attic flat. "Can't you find out for sure if you're pregnant or not?"

"I could have a test, I suppose. There's a place that advertises in the local paper. But it's too soon yet; I'll wait until I'm a month overdue."

"I can't wait that long." He lit a cigarette. "We're going on holiday tomorrow."

"Where to?"

"Down to the Isle of Wight for a week. I know I won't enjoy it; I'll be so worried all the time."

"What are you so worried about, anyway?" asked Lucy sulkily. "It's me who's having the baby – if I am having one – not you."

"But I feel so guilty; it's all my fault."

"It's just as much my fault. I wanted sex as much as you did."

"I'm so scared of my wife finding out."

"She won't. How could she?"

"Wouldn't you tell her?"

"Of course not. Why should I?"

"You'll need money for the child's maintenance, won't you?"

"I suppose so," agreed Lucy absently. "I hadn't thought of that."

"Well, I have. I can't understand why you're not as worried as I am."

"Maybe I really want the baby… Can you understand that?"

"No, I can't."

He sat puffing nervously at his cigarette, until Lucy asked in a small voice, "Don't you want to come to bed with me anymore?"

"Yes, I still want you alright." Joe laughed shortly and stubbed out his cigarette. "I've brought something with me tonight, so it'll be quite safe – that's if the damage isn't done already."

Afterwards, as they lay in bed together, Joe asked, "Can I phone you while I'm away?"

"Why bother? It'll only worry you if the answer's still no. I'll get a pregnancy test done, then I'll know next time I see you."

"Okay."

They got dressed, and Joe remarked grimly, "Well, I hope it'll be good news when I see you again."

"Send me a postcard."

He looked pained at her flippant tone. "Lucy, sometimes I just don't understand you," he sighed. "Goodbye."

He kissed her, and she knew everything was alright between them.

"Don't worry," she whispered against his cheek, "I won't tell your wife. Goodbye, Joe."

She was relieved to be free of him for a while, though she'd miss him in bed. She pondered on what he'd said. Yes, she would need money for the child, but she knew Joe earned only enough to keep his wife and child and pay the rent. Lucy didn't have much idea of money; she'd always had enough and a bit left over. Surely she'd manage alright? There was always social security.

She picked up the local newspaper and turned to the personal column. There it was: *"Pregnancy testing. Black's Laboratories, 4 Charlotte Street. Bring morning urine specimen. Same day service. Fee £2."*

She'd go next week. Every day she watched anxiously for her period to come... and would have been very disappointed if it had. She'd noticed a tight, tingling sensation in her breasts lately, but she didn't feel sick. She'd get the test done so she could be sure one way or the other.

She decided to go and have a look at Joe's house on Pains Road while he wasn't there, just for curiosity. She knew it was number 12, because he'd written his address on the letter he'd sent to her at Carnmisk. She walked up there on Sunday afternoon. Down by the railway it seemed grimy and tired on this hot afternoon in late summer. Grass on the embankments lay lank and smudged with diesel oil, where a few bedraggled dog daisies bloomed. Lucy plodded up the long road past the Rat's Castle, sleeping black and shuttered in the sunshine, and the air shimmered above patches of hot tar in the road.

Pains Road was one of the terraced brick streets up near the cornfield. Number twelve was no different from all the others – brown brick walls, sash windows, slate roof. Lucy thought of Joe living there with his wife and child. This was his home; all that was dear and precious to him was here in this mean little house.

She wandered up to the cornfield, which lay hairy pale gold in the sunshine, dotted with red poppies. Sitting on a stile, she surveyed the town in the valley below. She focussed her short-sighted eyes on the church tower in the High Street, and the tall grey houses climbing up Light Street on the hillside opposite her. She admired the flaxen shine on the cornfield, and the purple sheen on grass in the meadows.

Looking at the town of Redfold spread out below her, Lucy felt fond of it. It was her home now; she'd lived a much fuller life here in the last few months than in twenty-two years at Carnmisk. It wasn't just Joe; it also included the music and atmosphere at the Railway folk club, and her new friendship with Margaret. She'd be seeing Margaret on Tuesday, she thought happily as she slid off the stile to make her way home.

*

Sitting in Margaret's living room on Tuesday evening, Lucy asked diffidently, "Have you read my stories yet?"

"Yes, I liked them." There was a hesitancy in Margaret's voice that showed she had reservations. "Have you ever tried to get them published?"

"Yes, but they weren't accepted."

"I can understand why not," said Margaret gently. "You cram too much into them, too much description, too many words. You don't mind me saying what I think, do you?"

"No." Lucy was disappointed, but she knew Margaret was right. She loved words and couldn't bear to cut them out once she'd written them. "Well," she said resignedly, "I write to please myself, not to write what other people might want."

"But you'd like other people to enjoy your writing, wouldn't you? Why not put the stories aside for a year or two, then re-write them when you're a bit older and have more experience?"

"But I want to write now."

Margaret laughed kindly, and asked, "How old are you now?"

"Twenty-three."

"Well, you've got years yet, in which to write. You'll be a success at it one day, I have a feeling that you will."

Paul came in and agreed to go to bed, then Margaret made some coffee.

"Paul's been telling me a dirty joke he heard at school." She laughed. "Sometimes I wonder if the children respect me enough, the things they tell me."

"I think it's wonderful that they can say anything to you," observed Lucy. "I hope I'll be like that with mine… if I ever have any."

Margaret gave her a quizzical look, and asked, "Would you like to get married?"

"Yes… for security, I suppose, the security of knowing that whatever others think of me, there'd be someone who thinks enough of me to want to share his life with me."

"Yes," agreed Margaret. "I suppose I don't really care what other people think of me, because I know Ken loves me. How about putting an advert in the newspaper?" she joked.

"Don't tell anyone," Lucy grinned, "but I answered one of those adverts once!" She told Margaret about John Loat and Brian Hobden, and they had a good laugh over it all.

"Have you got a boyfriend now?" asked Margaret.

"No." Lucy wavered, then decided to tell her. "Well, actually I'm going out with a married man."

"Are you?" Margaret's voice was gentle.

"I'm not in love with him, but I like him a lot… his wife doesn't know. Do you think I'm horrible?"

"No." Margaret smiled. "Why should I?"

"Well, you seem so innocent, somehow. I thought you might think it's wrong of me to have an affair with a married man."

"Ken always says I'm innocent," Margaret laughed, "and sometimes I think the children know more than I do! But as long as you're not breaking up this man's marriage… though you could easily get hurt."

"No, I couldn't, I don't love him."

"Maybe you do really but think you don't."

"No, I'd know if I did." Lucy told Margaret about Samuel. She'd never told anyone about him before, except briefly to Joe. It was a relief to talk about it, even after all this time.

Walking back home down dim, privet-scented streets, Lucy came to a decision: she'd go to that place in Charlotte Street tomorrow and get the pregnancy test done. Up in her attic she put out a bowl and a brown glass bottle ready for the morning. *This time tomorrow I'll know for sure*, she told herself as she got into bed.

8
August

Lucy took the bottle and its contents to work next day. In the lunch hour she slipped down to the town on the bus and found Charlotte Street. It was a drab brown back street behind the farmers' market. Number 4 was a family-planning shop. Lucy entered furtively and handed the bottle to a woman at the counter, who gave Lucy a form to fill in, took the two pounds and told her to come back later for the result.

Lucy worked in a dream all afternoon. It was like waiting for an exam result, only she wasn't sure what result she really wanted. Five o'clock came at last, and she got the bus down to the town again. She entered the shop in Charlotte Street with beating heart. The woman handed back the brown bottle and an envelope, announcing impersonally, "We have a positive result for you, Miss Grey."

Lucy left the shop and walked up Light Street in a daze. She didn't know whether to be pleased or scared. *I'm going to be a mother!* she thought with an almost holy joy. *It's wonderful, amazing, yet the most natural thing in the world...*

Up in her attic, she opened the envelope. It contained a letter to give to her doctor, a leaflet entitled "Eating for two" and various advice. There was some information about how to obtain an abortion, but she didn't bother to read it. Nothing was going to stop her from having this baby!

The problem of telling her parents loomed at the back of her mind. She needn't do it yet; she wouldn't be seeing them until Christmas. She'd be about six months pregnant by then! The baby would probably be born sometime in March, she calculated.

She wrote the momentous news in her diary after tea, then went to bed early. She woke during the night and couldn't get back to sleep, so she got up and put a pan of milk on the stove to drink. While waiting for it to boil, she climbed up and opened the skylight to look out into the vast, calm silence of the night... Feeling suddenly small and vulnerable, she whispered, "Oh God, please be with me."

The stars looked aloof and far away, and Lucy wondered if God had heard her, or whether He was there at all... Some words for a poem came to her, which she scribbled down as she sipped the hot milk.

Then she lay down again, thinking with a thrill: *I'm not alone anymore: a new soul inhabits a tiny group of cells in my body, part of me yet not me.* She wondered whether it was a boy or a girl. She hoped it was a boy, though she didn't know why. If it was a boy she'd call him Samuel, after her first love. Maybe he'd inherit her writing talent and Joe's musical talent... maybe he'd be a famous author one day, and they'd write his biography and say how he'd inherited his talent from his mother... they might publish her diaries then...

Lucy pulled herself up sharply. She mustn't use the child just so she could shine in his reflected glory. He'd be a person in his own right; she mustn't try to plan his life for him, then be disappointed, as her father had in her. She wondered what colour his eyes would be. She hoped they'd be blue... it was impossible not to hope and dream of what he – or she – would be like.

She felt she must tell someone; she'd burst keeping such a stupendous thing to herself. It was difficult to catch Margaret alone at work, but as she was leaving at one o'clock next day, Lucy called to her softly, "Come here a minute... is Ken away any more evenings this week?"

"He's out on Thursday. Would you like to come and see me about something?"

"Yes, but I need to see you alone."

"Come tonight, Ken won't be in the way."

"No, it can wait."

"Is it something exciting?" asked Margaret, smiling. "You look pleased."

"Well, I think it's exciting, but I don't know if you will."

"It sounds interesting! Come and see me tomorrow, then."

*

Joe telephoned on Wednesday evening. Lucy raced downstairs every time it rang, worried it might be him, and this time it was. He was in a telephone box, and his voice followed anxiously after the pips.

"Lucy? Has it come?"

"No."

"Have you had a test done?"

"Well, I don't want to spoil your holiday."

"Lucy, for God's sake, tell me!"

She looked around to make sure there was nobody about, then she hissed into the telephone, "*I'm pregnant!*"

There was a groan at the other end. "Oh my God!"

"Don't worry!" said Lucy impatiently. "Don't let your wife see there's anything wrong. I told you I won't tell her."

The pips sounded, so Lucy told him to ring off; she'd see him next week.

Relieved that his phone call was over with, she retreated to her attic. She lay on the bed looking up at raindrops on the skylight. Then she remembered the book about babies she'd borrowed from the library on the way home. She picked it up and studied pictures of embryos in the womb. She was about six weeks pregnant, so it must have sprouted tiny arms and a tail already, and a huge head. She wondered what it thought of down in its warm dark cave, or whether it was aware of anything at all yet.

*

Next day the morning sickness started. Lucy couldn't touch cornflakes, so she tried a scrambled egg. She managed to cook it and eat it, then brought it back up again. *I hope this won't last too long*, she thought anxiously, *or the baby won't get any nourishment.*

It was a chilly grey evening when she went along to Blackdown Avenue. She was furious when she entered Margaret's living room and found the neighbour there. Catching Margaret's eye, she saw that she was aware of and amused by her anger. Lucy sat mutely fuming while the neighbour stayed gossiping for twenty minutes, then at last she went back next door.

"Well, what's your news?" asked Margaret, shutting the door. "Have you had a story published?"

"No, nothing like that... you know, I'm such a fool – when I've got something important to tell someone, my mouth slips about and I can't get the words out."

"Alright, I won't look at you while you say it!"

Lucy made an effort, then managed to announce in a shaky voice, "I'm pregnant."

Margaret spun round and stretched out her hand in sympathy, gasping, "Oh, Lucy!"

"It's alright," said Lucy hastily. "You needn't feel sorry for me – I'm pleased about it really. The father's that married man I told you about."

"I didn't realise you were having intercourse with him." Margaret still hadn't recovered from her amazement.

"Do I seem so innocent, then?" asked Lucy wryly.

"It's just that it's so difficult to imagine you getting so far in a relationship with someone as to have intercourse."

"Well, I've managed to make a relationship with you, haven't I?"

"Yes, but I'm not a man! Does he know you're pregnant?"

"Yes. He's worried stiff that I'll tell his wife, but I won't. There wouldn't be any point in it, as I don't love him."

"No. Would you marry him if he was divorced?"

"No. I like him and I'm attracted to him, but he irritates me. Do you think I'm wicked going to bed with a man I don't love?"

"No, you obviously have some feelings for him. But what are you going to do with the baby?"

"Keep it, of course."

"Yes, it's natural that you want to, but where are you going to live with it?"

"I don't know… I hope I'll be able to go home to my parents to have it."

"How will they take it?"

"They'll be horrified." Lucy shuddered. "I dread having to tell them."

"And how will you manage about money?"

"Social security, I suppose. I'll have to see a social worker about the practical side of things. Can you understand that I want the baby?"

"Yes, but I don't think you realise all the problems it could involve. Have you seen a doctor yet?"

"No, I suppose I'd better…"

*

It wasn't too bad seeing the doctor on Friday evening. She was a brisk youngish woman who didn't preach at

August

Lucy, just asked whether she would keep the baby or not. "It should be born about 17th March next year," said the doctor, consulting a list of dates. Lucy explained that she'd be going home to Cornwall for the birth.

Of course, she reflected as she walked up Light Street, that would depend upon her parents accepting her. Surely they would. She was their daughter, whatever she'd done. She'd once accused her father of being ashamed of her because she hadn't qualified in a professional career. He had denied this, assuring her that he'd never be ashamed of her, whatever she did. Well, soon she'd see if he'd meant it.

It was a dull, heavy August evening. Lucy wished it would either rain or clear, instead of that murky, liverish sky. The telephone was ringing as she opened Crimmond's door.

"Hello? Lucy?" It was Joe. "We're coming back tomorrow, so I'll come and see you Sunday evening."

"Alright. You haven't been worrying too much, have you?"

"Oh no!" His voice was sarcastic. "Like hell I have!" The pips sounded. "See you Sunday."

*

The weather cleared on Sunday. In the afternoon Lucy walked down by the river, where bright dragonflies like blue needles skimmed between brown velvet bulrushes, and algae lay on the water like green paint on glass. She wasn't looking forward to seeing Joe later; he'd probably be all worked up.

He was even worse than she'd expected. He stood haggard and dreary-eyed on the doorstep, looking like he hadn't slept for a week. Up in the attic, he slumped in the chair and burst out, "If only you knew the mental anguish I've gone through! I've forced myself to smile and be normal, but I could go and throw myself in the sea for what I've done to you."

"But—" protested Lucy.

"My life is in your hands," he declared dramatically. "I'll lose everything if my wife finds out. Her father owns our house, so if she throws me out I'll be homeless."

Tears rained down his cheeks, and Lucy felt compassion mixed with scorn. He was like a wretched little boy. "Come here," she said gently, sitting on the chair's arm and drawing Joe's head to her breast.

"If I was single I'd marry you," he sobbed. "Then I could be satisfied I'd done the right thing."

Lucy felt hurt. It would have been kinder of him to say he'd marry her because he loved her, not just to satisfy his conscience. But she didn't love him, so how could she expect him to love her, or even pretend to? Well, she'd be honest too.

"I wouldn't marry you," she said.

"Why not?" He looked up in surprise. "Because you'd think I could be deceitful?"

"No, not that. But, much as I like you, I wouldn't want to spend the rest of my life with you. I don't love you, any more than you love me."

He didn't deny this, and exclaimed, "I'll think of you for the rest of my life. How can you forgive me for doing this to you?"

"I don't bear you any grudge," replied Lucy, absently twining his hair round her finger. "I wanted sex as much as you did. You gave me pleasure and affection when I needed it. What good would it do me to tell your wife? If she divorces you, I don't want you. Why break up a marriage for nothing? I don't want to be cited as co-respondent in a divorce case! Anyway, I want the baby really."

Joe looked up at her dumbly, his hazel eyes flooded with relief. Then he made his speech. "For your sincerity, your beauty and your grace, I'm glad it was you. Thank God for your integrity. Thank God you're adult and sensible, not a silly, screaming teenager demanding money or to see my wife. I'll always be beholden to you for not destroying me. You have my deepest concern. The man who marries you will be lucky; I hope he realises it."

All very fine, thought Lucy sourly, *but it's just words.* She was glad he didn't suggest getting into bed; she didn't feel like it when she despised him. *Why do I despise him?* she asked herself after he'd gone. Because he was weak, breaking down and blubbing like a little boy. God knew she was weak enough herself in many ways, but she was the kind of woman who needed a man to be stronger than herself.

Why was she so adamant that his wife shouldn't find out? Was it all concern for Joe, and shrinking from being involved in a possible divorce? No, it was her sense of justice. She'd wanted everything he'd given her, including the baby. Was she to repay him by ruining his marriage? And she had no reason to hurt his wife and child, either. If she did wreak havoc in the lives of these three people, she knew she'd feel mean and low down about it for the rest of her life.

She frowned, remembering Joe's words just now. All his concern was for himself, that his wife mustn't find out. That was only natural, but he might have asked how she'd manage, or how she was feeling. She'd been feeling pretty grotty these last couple of days. The only sustenance she could keep down were glucose drinks and yogurt.

*

She dragged herself to work next day, feeling tired and empty. At tea break Mrs Browning asked was she alright, as she looked so white and drawn. Lucy brushed off this enquiry, grimacing comically at Margaret.

She told Margaret all about Joe's reactions next time she went to visit, and Margaret remarked, "Maybe it's just as well that you despise him now, and assure yourself that you don't care about him anymore, otherwise you might remember him as better than he is, and hanker after him."

"One thing." It suddenly occurred to Lucy. "He didn't suggest I should have an abortion."

"Have you thought of having one?"

"No. Not for any moral reason, but because I want the baby."

"Have you seen a doctor yet?"

"Yes." Lucy spoke of returning to Cornwall to have the baby, if her parents allowed it.

"You're sure they will?"

"Yes, I think so. They'll say some hard things, of course, but I'm sure they won't cast me off their doorstep!"

"Well, if they do, then you're welcome to have the baby and convalesce here in our house until you can find somewhere," offered Margaret.

Lucy was surprised and touched by her friend's generosity. "I couldn't do that," she murmured, "but it's very kind of you to offer." She searched her mind for something she could do for Margaret. "I'll babysit for you any time, you know," she suggested.

"Good, I might take you up on that! Have you started knitting for the baby yet?"

"No, I haven't thought about it. What shall I knit?"

Margaret fetched some knitting patterns, which they browsed through together.

"I'll knit three jerseys," declared Lucy. "One in blue, one in green and one in lilac."

"Lucy!" exclaimed Margaret in mock horror. "You can't dress a new baby in all colours of the rainbow! Newborn babies always wear white."

"I don't like white," protested Lucy, "it's boring. Alright, a nice warm cream then, but I must knit one blue one, because I'm sure it's going to be a boy."

They talked about childbirth, and Margaret assured Lucy she had nothing to fear.

A full moon hung low in the sky as Lucy walked home through the shadowy streets. It was bright and round as a lemon drop, and Lucy rejoiced that she too was full and ripe – she was a woman and she was going to bear a child.

9
September

Joe didn't come again until the middle of September. He glanced fearfully at Lucy's figure as she opened the door.

"It's alright, it doesn't show yet," she said brusquely. "Have you been too scared to come and see me all this time?"

"I've been ill." He slumped dejectedly into her chair upstairs. "I've been so depressed. In the early mornings I sit in my van waiting for the petrol to fill up, and I look up at the stars and want to cry. I went to see a doctor the other day and just burst into tears. He prescribed some anti-depressant pills for me."

"You didn't tell him about me, did you?"

"No, I haven't told anyone. There's no-one I can tell."

"Only me. But why are you so depressed? You know I won't tell your wife. Don't you trust me?"

"I'm worried you might change your mind."

"I won't," said Lucy shortly. "You can do me a favour too. Don't ever make yourself known to my parents. They'll just think of you as an anonymous man who seduced their daughter, but if they saw you it would be more real to them. I don't suppose you ever will, of course."

"No danger of that," muttered Joe. "Is your father a violent man?"

"He could be if he was really roused. But I won't tell him who you are. I'll just say you're a married man; that's all that needs to be said."

To her surprise she agreed to get into bed. She found she didn't enjoy it with him anymore. The romance – if there had ever been any – had died. *There has to be romance in it*, she realised, *otherwise it's nothing, like eating a meal when you're not hungry.*

When they lay together afterwards, Lucy asked curiously, "Are your parents still alive?"

"Why?" asked Joe, immediately suspicious.

"It's alright," she said impatiently, "I'm not going to tell them. I just feel an interest in them as my child's grandparents."

"My mother's still alive," he replied. "She's Irish; she lives in a flat on the new estate north of the town. My father died a couple of years ago, back in Somerset. He was a hard man; he used to beat my mother before he left us. She had four of us to bring up alone. It was very difficult for her – sometimes we didn't get enough to eat."

"What was your father's job?"

"He was a plasterer, and a very artistic one too. He was quite a handsome man."

"I hope the baby will be a boy."

"Boys can be more trouble to bring up… I must go now. I'll drop in again and see you some time. Goodbye, Lucy."

He kissed her tenderly, and she felt she liked him again.

"Goodbye Joe," she kissed him back, "and *don't worry!* You can trust me."

"Yes, I know I can," he whispered into her hair. "You're truly a wonderful person."

He was gone, and she was glad. She felt she never wanted to see him again. *He still didn't ask how I'll manage with the baby*, she thought resentfully, *or how I'm feeling.*

She was feeling better now. The sickness had passed, but there were other complications. "I'll never laugh at jokes about constipation again!" she vowed, slamming the toilet door behind her after a futile ten minutes in there one morning. Her kitchen cupboard was like a health store now. There were jars of honey, rosehip syrup, cod liver oil, yeast extract… all sorts of things that she dosed herself with every day. *This is going to be the strongest, healthiest, most beautiful baby that's ever been born*, she vowed fiercely.

Sometimes she worried that things might go wrong. She felt that she'd kill herself if she lost the baby by miscarriage. Why? Because she'd pinned all her hopes on it; the baby was her reason for living now, and if she lost it her life would be even emptier than before. She knew it would be colossally selfish to kill herself, knowing the grief it would cause her parents. But the thought of living on alone – with no child, no husband, no interest in her job, growing more sour and neurotic – frightened her. She just couldn't face it. She realised there might be dangers in suicide, that she might end up in black nothingness or find herself in a worse spiritual place, but she still felt she'd do it.

She was turning these thoughts over in her mind in bed one night, trying to sleep in spite of the noise below. A bunch of what her father would have called "trendy weirdos", with fuzzy beards, beads and ragged jeans, had recently moved into the flat downstairs. They had a liking for loud pop music… no, it wasn't pop music; what was it they called it? Progressive pop, that was it. It was an unmusical jangle of sounds and a beat, beat, beat that was driving Lucy mad. She was angry at their thoughtlessness, keeping her awake after midnight. The arrogance of them! Should she bang on the floor? She must assert herself; she'd be a mug to put up with it. She pulled a boot from under the bed and banged it three times on the floor.

She heard laughter, then suddenly the music got very loud. Oh, so they were answering back, were they? Lucy sprang out of bed, furious. She'd go down there and complain, and to hell with being scared! Just as she reached the door the noise was turned down. It was still audible, but only just. Grimly satisfied, Lucy went back to bed.

*

Next day she had an appointment with a social worker, in the social services office in a red brick lodge by the river. It was a crisp autumn afternoon, with willow leaves in yellow drifts along the riverbank. Lucy found herself looking speculatively at babies in prams. *Mostly they're ugly little beings*, she thought, *with faces like pink prunes.* Hers wouldn't look like that, of course.

Entering the lodge, she was directed to an office room to see a Miss Fry. Miss Fry had a crisp, chilly manner that immediately intimidated Lucy. She imagined her visiting the poorer homes of Redfold with her cold eyes and precise voice, getting people's backs up and making them feel inferior. *She's probably got half a dozen degrees and letters after her name*, thought Lucy, *but she's useless at connecting with people and putting them at ease.*

"Why do you want to keep the baby?" asked Miss Fry.

Lucy stared at her. What a question! "Because I'm its mother, of course."

Miss Fry advised her to get on to Redfold's housing list as soon as possible, although it could take years before she'd be offered a council house or flat. She could also apply for a flat in a special block for one-parent families, for which there was a long waiting list.

Walking back afterwards, Lucy felt depressed. She hoped it wouldn't be too difficult to return to Redfold with the baby. She didn't want to stay at home with the baby and her parents for years. She realised that her parents wouldn't like it either.

Ruth knocked on her door that evening. "Lucy," she called, "I've got some sugar I owe you."

She came in and dumped a bag of sugar on the table, observing, "That looks nice, it's a baby's jacket, isn't it?"

Lucy dropped her blue knitting guiltily. She'd forgotten

to hide it before Ruth came in. Well, she might as well tell her; she'd notice soon enough anyway.

"Whose baby is it for?" asked Ruth absently, not really interested.

"Mine." Lucy lowered her eyes and tried to control her mouth.

"Eh?" Ruth stared at her. "You're joking, aren't you?"

"No, it's due in March."

"Well! I'd never have believed it!"

"Why not?"

"You're so quiet, you never seem to go out much or have any boyfriends."

"I'm still human, even if I am quiet." Lucy was rather nettled. "I've got the same feelings as anyone else."

"Do you know who the father is?"

"Of course I know who he is!" Lucy was annoyed.

"Won't he marry you?"

"He's married already," admitted Lucy, "and I don't want his wife to find out."

"Why not?"

"I don't want to get him into trouble."

"But he's got you into trouble."

"No, it takes two. Anyway, it's not trouble, I want the baby."

"Do you?" Ruth regarded her curiously. "How will you manage?"

"Go home to my parents for a while, I suppose."

"How will they like that?"

"Not much. I haven't told them yet."

"How did you meet the father – or shouldn't I ask?"

"At a party. Not the one you took me to, but another one," Lucy lied hastily.

"But didn't you take any precautions?"

"Yes, but it didn't work."

"Oh. Is he going to pay you any maintenance for the baby?"

"No, he can't afford it."

"Hmph, that's what he says, I suppose. You'll find it difficult on just social security. Have you told Mrs Ashby yet?"

"No."

"Well, if I were you I'd tell her before it shows."

Lucy was somewhat put out. Ruth had made her feel like a naughty child who'd done something stupid, instead of a fellow woman of the world. Well, she'd told her now, and got it over with. She wondered how she'd manage to tell them at work. There'd been a chance that morning, but she'd backed out. Ginny, one of the girl clerical assistants, had asked her to help move a filing cabinet because she'd dropped a comb behind it. Lucy had stood up, ready to oblige, when she'd suddenly remembered that the risk of miscarriage is greatest in the third month of pregnancy. Would she risk her baby just to please this silly girl? Of course not! "I've got a bad back," she stammered. "I can't do anything heavy at the moment."

"Oh." Ginny stared at her with round light eyes, then flounced back to her companions, from where Lucy heard muffled mutterings and exclamations. *I suppose Mrs Browning will ask kindly after my back now*, she thought crossly. She couldn't stand Ginny, who was so fluffily feminine she was almost kittenish. Ginny was engaged, of course, with a dainty diamond ring on her finger, always chattering about "Marty" in laborious detail.

Lucy went for a walk by the golf course as usual in the lunch hour, in the golden September weather. *There's a sadness about autumn*, she reflected, *despite the brave colours – the woolly gold chestnut trees, russet beeches and rose hips like little scarlet eggs.* She picked up the first conker of the season, as shiny brown as if polished. Some poetic words came to her, which she scribbled down in a notebook in her bag.

Back in the office Lucy slunk to her corner, conscious of curious glances from the clerical assistants' desks. Mrs Browning didn't notice her. That lady was holding up a new pair of pants she'd just bought in the town for her husband, for the other women to admire. Lucy grinned as she wondered how Mr Browning would feel about this display of his underwear.

Later on, Mrs Browning padded round to Lucy's corner and asked solicitously, "How's your back, Lucy, dear?"

"Not so bad," grunted Lucy. "How's your husband's?"

Mr Browning's lumbago was one of his wife's favourite subjects, and her bovine eyes beamed as she described it in detail. *Well*, thought Lucy, *at least I've diverted her attention from me.* She wondered how long it would be before anyone noticed her pregnancy. There was no change in her figure yet, except that her belly was quite firm and rounded.

"How am I going to tell them at work?" she asked Margaret over coffee one evening.

"I'll tell them if you like," suggested Margaret.

"But I'm always there when you're there," objected Lucy. "I suppose I could go down to the loo for five minutes or so while you tell them."

"Don't plan things," Margaret laughed, "just let them happen. I'll find the right moment. When are you going to tell your parents?"

"I don't know… I keep putting it off."

"Will they take it very badly?"

"Yes, they will, but I just can't imagine what they'll say. I've never been able to talk to them about such things. My mother gave me a book about the facts of life when I was twelve, but we never talked about it. Could you with your parents?"

"No," replied Margaret, "it's natural to be embarrassed with parents about sex. I'm sure most parents just blindly hope that their children will be alright, without their having to say anything on the subject."

"Yes," agreed Lucy. "I suppose parents and relatives think you're pure and innocent in that way just because you're their child. I remember once I overheard my grandmother grumbling to my mother about the promiscuity of modern girls, then she said comfortably, 'Lucy's not like that, of course.' For all she knew I could be on the pill and sleeping with a different bloke every night!"

"What will she say now?"

"She died last year, so she'll be spared the shock!"

A light mist was forming as Lucy walked back in the dusk, and there was a chill in the air. Summer was definitely over now; she could almost smell the approach of winter.

Winter... she'd be seeing her parents at Christmas... she pushed the thought away and breathed in the scent of woodsmoke from a garden bonfire.

When Mrs Ashby came to collect the rent that week, Lucy remembered what Ruth had said. *I'd better tell her now*, she decided. She knew that Mrs Ashby was a keen churchwoman, but whether she'd take a charitable or condemnatory view of the situation, Lucy wasn't sure. She tried to speak while her landlady was in the room, but the words wouldn't come. Mrs Ashby turned to the doorway, and Lucy told herself, *Come on, it's got to be done.*

"Mrs Ashby," she called. "I'd better tell you something."

She heard Ruth's door click open. Mrs Ashby turned her bulk (she was quite a large lady) back to Lucy and asked, "Well?"

"I'd better tell you... that I'm pregnant." The words were out, and Lucy felt relieved.

"Oh." Mrs Ashby's eyes swept coldly over Lucy's figure. "Are you getting married?"

"No."

"Indeed. Well, I must say you've been very silly, and you're just beginning to pay for it. Has the man been up here with you?"

"Yes... sometimes."

"You'd better not let him in here again then. I'll let you stay here until you leave; if I evicted you now you'd have a terrible job finding other accommodation, in your predicament. You will be leaving, I trust?"

"Yes, I'll go home to my parents."

"What will you live on?"

"Social security."

"That's meant for people in real need. They might not consider you; you've got yourself into that state. Anyway, that's your affair," she concluded curtly. "Goodnight."

"Phew!" exclaimed Ruth, making no secret of her eavesdropping. "Nasty woman! She's just jealous because you've had a good time."

"But she can have a good time whenever she likes."

"Ah, it's not the same when you're married! What's that you're eating?" She looked distastefully at Lucy's tea on the table.

"Stewed sheep's brains on toast," replied Lucy. "It's full of protein, good for the baby."

"Yeuk!" Ruth retreated back to her room.

Lucy shut her door. She felt a primitive pride in her pregnancy, in spite of her landlady's disapproval. She sprinkled salt and pepper on her meal and sat down to eat.

10

October

One morning in October a dense white mist lay in the valley of Redfold, holding up traffic and buses. This made Lucy twenty minutes late for work. By the sudden hush which fell on the office room as she entered, she realised that Margaret had told them of her pregnancy. Her heart thumped very fast, and she hoped no-one would speak to her until she could calm down. Charlie Radlett appeared, gave her a puzzled look and an awkward "Good morning", seemed unsure whether or not to sit down, then lumbered out again.

Oh, so he knew too then. But why was he so embarrassed? If it had been Ginny or any of the other girls, he'd have been all fatherly. *I know why*, decided Lucy. *To him I seem such an aloof, reserved, cold person that he finds it impossible to imagine me surrendering in bed to any man, therefore to him it seems indecent.*

Ginny came pattering round to Lucy's corner, her round eyes bright with curiosity. She'd only come to put a file away in the cabinet, and Lucy was relieved when she didn't say anything. Nobody said anything to her all day, not even Mrs Browning, though Lucy was conscious of many surreptitious glances.

"Well, what did they say?" she asked Margaret over coffee that evening.

"They were absolutely flabbergasted!" Margaret laughed. "They just couldn't believe it at first. They said what a shame it was, as you're such a quiet, reserved girl."

"Oh, so they're taking that attitude, are they?" grimaced Lucy. "I'm a 'nice' girl who's been seduced by a 'wicked' man, so they feel sorry for me. Did they ask about the father?"

"Yes, but I just said you hadn't told me much about him. I told them you're pleased, which surprised them even more! They admire you for wanting to keep the baby."

"Why?" puzzled Lucy. "Why do people think an unmarried mother is good and heroic if she keeps her baby, and selfish if she gives it away? It's the other way round, really. I'm selfish because I want to keep him, when he might have a better life with a couple who can give him a normal family life. It must take a great deal of heroic unselfishness to give up a child – for its own good – that you've just given birth to."

"Yes, but do you really think the baby would be better off adopted, away from you?"

"I like to think I'm the best one to bring him up, being his natural mother. But I can't give him a father."

October

"You might get married one day."

"No, I won't," said Lucy definitely. "I'm not the type that gets married; I'm too insular and awkward. But it doesn't bother me so much now, because I'll have the baby. I suppose a child and no husband is better than having neither!"

She felt strong and well as she strolled along the damp turf by the golf course in the lunch hour next day. *This is the most comfortable time of pregnancy*, she decided. *I'm past the first few months' sickness but haven't reached the ungainly heaviness of the last couple of months yet.* The chestnut trees looked sad and bedraggled after a night's rain, their yellow leaves hanging limply, like wet bananas.

Back in the office, she glanced through Charlie's local newspaper. She hadn't visited the Railway folk club lately, so she looked to see who would be performing there on Thursday evening… "The Earthy Grunt Band". That sounded like the noises that emanated up from the downstairs flat at night. They didn't trouble her so much now; she seemed to have an unspoken agreement with them to turn the noise down after 11pm. She'd try this Earthy Grunt Band tomorrow evening; she felt like going out somewhere.

*

The autumn evenings were chill now, and Lucy shivered as she hurried down to the Railway folk club next evening. The Earthy Grunt Band were a group of four shaggy-haired boys who produced weird sounds with spoons, pots, saucepans and bicycle bells. They made a terrible din, but they had vitality, and Lucy found herself enjoying it after a while.

She wondered if the baby was listening, hidden away in its dark cocoon. She'd read a theory somewhere that babies grow up liking whatever music they hear while in their mothers' wombs. She'd grumbled to Margaret on Tuesday evening, "With all that racket coming up from downstairs every night, he'll grow up liking progressive pop music."

"Well," Margaret had replied, "if he – or she – wants to like progressive pop music when he grows up, then it's his affair, not yours!"

"Yes, I know I mustn't try to impose my tastes on him, but it'll be good for our relationship if we like the same things."

Still, the sounds of the Earthy Grunt Band weren't unmusical. There was a short interval when they'd finished, and a boy sitting next to Lucy remarked, "I think they're fantastic, don't you?"

"Not sure, really," replied Lucy hesitantly. "They're not bad."

"I'll be singing after the interval," he indicated his guitar, "but I'm only a floor singer."

"Oh. What's that?"

"I don't get paid for it!"

He was a slight pale boy with eager eyes. Lucy wondered what his songs were like and watched with interest as he climbed up on the stage and perched on a stool with his guitar.

"I'll sing a song I wrote the other day," he announced, without a trace of nervousness. He had difficulty finding the right note to start, then he launched into a rather feeble, very sentimental song, with his voice squeaking on the high notes. Lucy felt embarrassed for him. There was a trickle of applause when he'd finished, and Lucy expected him to slink off the stage in shame at his poor performance. But as he clambered back beside her he said jauntily, "There, that wasn't bad, was it?"

Lucy muttered something non-committal, and the boy introduced himself. "My name's Timothy, by the way. Call me Tim. Can I buy you a drink?"

Lucy asked for her usual ginger wine.

"What's your name?" Tim asked as they sat with their drinks.

"Lucy."

"Has anyone ever told you you're very pretty?"

Pause, then, "Yes."

"Like me to walk home with you?"

"Alright," agreed Lucy in surprise. It seemed odd that this boy should show an interest in her when she was carrying another man's child. But, of course, he couldn't know.

As they walked through the dark chilly streets, Tim asked, "How old are you?"

"Twenty-three."

"Really? I thought you were about eighteen."

"I feel about eighteen sometimes."

"You're eighteen to me, Lucy." He caught up her hand and squeezed it. "Do you often go to the Railway by yourself?"

"Yes."

"You shouldn't, it's dangerous for a girl to walk alone through the streets at night."

"Well, nothing's happened to me yet."

"Ah, but it might. If anything happened to you, and you were in hospital, I'd sit by your bedside day and night."

"You'd soon get fed up with that!" Lucy laughed. "Anyway, the nurses would chuck you out."

A big yellow moon beamed down as they strolled along. Lucy smiled back at it, as if sharing a joke.

"Being involved hits you," observed Tim, as they climbed Light Street. "I feel I've known you all my life. Will you come out with me tomorrow night?"

"Where?"

"Just for a walk in the park."

Lucy pondered. *Well, why not? It'll be somewhere to go, and he'll soon lose interest when he knows I'm pregnant. Should I tell him now? No, it's half past ten and I'm tired. I'll tell him tomorrow.*

"Alright, I'll come," she promised.

"Good, meet me at the park gates at eight." He gazed after her as she stepped up to Crimmond's front door.

*

She thought how young and boyish he looked when she saw him waiting there next evening.

"You've come, then." He took her hand.

"Yes," she replied, "I said I would."

They sat down on a park bench.

"It's just us and the stars," observed Tim, putting his arm around her shoulders.

"That sounds romantic!" Lucy laughed.

"I think I love you," said Tim quietly.

"You can't," protested Lucy. "You've only known me two days."

"I still love you. Can't I make you love me?"

"You can't force it."

"If I went away, and you never saw me again, would you forget me?"

"Probably."

"Will you let me kiss you?"

"Would it mean a lot to you?"

"Yes, you know it would."

"Alright," sighed Lucy patiently. "Go on then."

He kissed her, very awkwardly.

"It's no good." Lucy stifled a desire to wipe her mouth. "It leaves me cold."

"What's wrong with me?"

"Nothing, you just don't turn me on. How old are you?"

"Nineteen."

"I'm much too old for you, you know."

"No, you're not." He took up her left hand. "Ever thought of wearing a ring on this finger? We could get engaged."

"No, I couldn't, I don't love you." She frowned in the autumn dusk, then decided she'd better tell him. "And I'm pregnant."

"Are you?" he squeaked incredulously. "You're not, you can't be."

"Why not?"

"Well…" He fumbled for words. "You… you're not that type."

"Anyone can be 'that type' if circumstances make them so."

"Who did it?"

"A married man."

"Does he know?"

"Yes."

"Is he going to help you?"

"No. I don't want his wife to find out."

"Why not?" Tim was surprised. "Why not make him suffer? He comes along and knocks you up, and you're letting him get away with it."

"Ah, but I wanted him to 'knock me up', so I can't very well pretend that he's injured me."

"Oh." Tim looked puzzled, then he insisted, "Look here, I still want to carry on seeing you. It doesn't make any difference. Come round to my place for tea tomorrow, then we'll watch that new film at the Regal afterwards."

"But you can't go out with me when I'm pregnant!" protested Lucy. "What will your parents think?"

"They won't notice. I didn't."

"No, but your mother might."

In the end she agreed to go. She laughed wryly to herself as she walked up Light Street. She didn't even feel flattered at someone saying he loved her at last, because she knew he didn't mean it. *Oh, he thinks he means it,* she thought sourly, *but he's just carried away with the romantic idea of "being in love". He'll probably kick himself when he wakes up tomorrow morning and remembers the things he said.*

The whole episode seemed ludicrous. It shed a new light on her feelings for Samuel. If he'd known, would he have despised her, and felt amused and irritated, as she did now with Tim? *Life is perverse*, she reflected as she climbed up to her attic. *When I want someone he doesn't want me, then when someone wants me I don't want him.*

Tim lived near the top of a big yellow brick block of flats in an estate in the north area of Redfold. It was a windy grey day as Lucy caught the bus to this area, where she'd never been before. She thought how ugly and barren it was, very different from the gracious, shrubby roads around Light Street. *Joe's mother lives here somewhere*, she reflected as she trod a concrete weal across a desolate wasteland of muddy grass between the vast blocks of flats. *My child's grandmother.*

She'd put on a loosely fitting pink corduroy smock dress, hoping Tim's mother wouldn't notice anything. She found the block where he lived. It was cold and eerie going up in the lift. The wind moaned around the building, and green lighted numbers of each floor appeared and disappeared as she went up and up. At last she stopped on the seventeenth floor, relieved to get out.

She was also relieved when Tim opened his door and told her, "My parents are out. They were going out anyway, but I'd forgotten. My mum's left us some tea."

Lucy detected an awkwardness in his manner. Obviously he regretted last night. She wondered whether he'd pretend nothing had happened.

"Miss me?" he asked as they sat down on the sofa.

"No."

"I made a fool of myself last night. I laughed about it this morning."

"Yes," agreed Lucy. "You said things you didn't mean."

"Well, it's not that I didn't mean them, but I was silly to say them like that."

They listened to some records, then had tea.

"Are you keeping the baby?" asked Tim diffidently.

"Yes."

"Aren't you afraid it'll spoil your chances of marriage?"

"I've never had any chances of marriage," said Lucy bitterly, "nor ever will have. Not because of the baby but because of my personality."

"Oh." Tim looked puzzled. "What's wrong with it?"

"Oh, lots of things…" She didn't feel like saying any more about it. "What time does the film start?"

It was a popular love story, which Lucy found a bit sloppy. Tim had already seen it before and kept her informed, in loud whispers, of what would happen next. She wasn't particularly interested in the film but was eventually so irritated by his whispering that she turned to him and hissed, "Shut up, I'm trying to listen!"

Out in the windy street afterwards, Tim said awkwardly, "Well, I hope you get home alright. Give me your phone number and I'll ring you sometime."

Knowing he wouldn't, Lucy wrote it down for him, said goodbye and walked off to the bus stop.

*

She told Margaret all about him the following Tuesday evening.

"Aren't some men ridiculously sentimental!" Lucy concluded the story. "He meets a girl he likes the look of, imagines he's in love with her after only two meetings, then decides they'll get engaged and live happy ever after. If I'd said yes, he'd have been stuck with me – and the baby – for the rest of his life, or until one of us ran off, without knowing what I'm really like."

"That would have been a catastrophe for him, indeed!" Margaret smiled. "But you never know, he might be suffering like you did over Samuel."

"No, he can't be," said Lucy definitely. "You can't be in love after a couple of evenings out with someone you hardly know. He's probably relieved now at getting out of an awkward situation!"

Margaret went into the kitchen to make some more coffee. As they sat sipping it, she asked, "Has Joe been round to see you lately?"

"No... I don't really want him to, but I wish he would, just to reassure me he's alright and hasn't broken down and told his wife."

"Maybe he's afraid to come," suggested Margaret. "If he actually sees your bump, it'll be more real to him that he's made you pregnant."

"Maybe. But it doesn't show that much yet, does it?"

"Well, you're not exactly flat anymore! I'll make you a maternity dress if you choose some material."

"Would you?" Lucy was pleased, as Margaret had a flair for dressmaking, and made clothes for her children.

"You know," observed Lucy, "you make it seem like fun having children, but some women made it seem like hard work."

"It is hard work! But it's fun too."

It had rained during the evening, and the pavements were plastered with wet leaves. Lucy trod carefully, afraid of slipping over and hurting her child. She often saw everything as a vague threat to her child. She'd hold her shopping bag like a shield in case anyone might brush against her in the street, and regarded steps and stairs as deliberately conspiring to trip her up. She felt like a fierce female animal, ready to attack anyone or anything that might hurt the child growing within her.

She smiled tenderly as she thought of him tucked away in there. She just couldn't think of it as "it". It was "him", she knew, as surely as if he'd been able to tell her so.

11

November

One evening in November Lucy was lying on her bed reading, when she felt a little tickle inside her. She dismissed it as indigestion, but it persisted, until she suddenly realised that this was the "quickening" – the baby was beginning to wriggle and kick in his warm little place. Lucy was thrilled. It was wonderful, almost as if he was communicating to let her know he was there.

Joe hadn't been round again since that evening in September. Lucy didn't really want to see him, but she felt hurt and angry. Did he blindly think she could be swept away under the carpet by being ignored? No, he was afraid, as Margaret had said, afraid of seeing her pregnancy, afraid of what she might demand of him. He still didn't quite trust her. She pictured him cowering in his house on Pains Road, worried every time the doorbell rang that it might be Lucy come to tell his wife. Yet he had only to come and see her, or even just to phone, to be reassured that she wouldn't.

What was it he'd said in a moment of sentiment in bed? "I'd like to give you a child; it would be like having two families." Obviously he hadn't thought through what he was saying. *There must have been some affection between us*, reflected Lucy, *because I don't dislike the thought of carrying his child... but I don't really think of the baby as Joe's at all – he's mine, made inside my flesh and blood, even though he's got some of Joe's genes.*

As if in answer to these thoughts, there was a letter from Joe next morning. It wasn't as long or as flowery as the last one he'd sent her, just a short note:

"Dear Lucy,

Please don't think I've forgotten you, because I haven't. I have been off sick from work, so I haven't been able to come and see you, but I think about you a lot.

Yours,

Joe."

I bet you do! Lucy smiled wryly. But she felt better. He'd acknowledged her existence, and tried, in his clumsy way, to show that he cared.

There still seemed to be a conspiracy of silence at work over her pregnancy, though they probably didn't know what to say. Mrs Browning had crept around to her corner one morning and whispered, "Lucy, dear, do you hope for a boy or a girl?"

"A boy."

"Right, I'll knit you a little jacket in blue."

Lucy was pleased and touched. They weren't such a bad crowd; she wished she could communicate better with them. She expressed this to Margaret one evening over coffee, and Margaret observed, "You're funny, you're two people really. One of you can laugh and chat with me here, but the other sits stiff and silent in the office all day."

"That's because I can blossom out when I'm with you," explained Lucy. "We're on the same wavelength, but I can't feel like that with them at work."

"Perhaps why it is," said Margaret thoughtfully, "is that people communicate with each other on various levels. Lots of people – particularly housewives – chat on household and small-talk levels. It's only with real friends and some family that the levels are deeper, and people's true selves communicate. Maybe you haven't got any social levels; you've only got your real self to offer, so you can only communicate with a very few people."

"Sometimes I wish we were all dumb," remarked Lucy, "and could only communicate with pencils and notebooks that we'd carry around all the time, like someone I used to know who stuttered badly. I feel so much more confident with my pen than with my tongue."

Margaret sewed in silence for a while, then she announced, "I've nearly finished your dress now. Try it on so I can adjust the hem… There, you look like Alice in Wonderland."

"I feel like a tent walking along."

"You'll soon fill it out." Margaret laughed. "You'll feel

like a cliff walking along in a few months' time! When are you seeing your parents?"

"Christmas… I suppose I'll have to write and tell them soon."

Yes, she told herself as she walked back through lamplit fog, *I can't put it off any longer. I'll do it tomorrow.*

*

Usually Lucy enjoyed writing letters, but the following evening she sat down to the task before her with extreme reluctance. Eventually she braced herself and wrote:

"Dear Mum and Dad,

I have some news for you. I am expecting a baby in March. I know that, with your standards, this will upset you a lot, and I'm very sorry.

I hope to keep the baby. The father is married. I don't want to break up his marriage by telling his wife and demanding maintenance.

Would it be alright if I come home and have the baby in hospital there, stay a few months with you until it's weaned, then return with it to Redfold? I am on the list for a one-parent-family flat here, so I'll live on social security until the baby is older and I can work again. There is a nursery attached to the flats where the child can be looked after while I'm at work.

I hope to be home for Christmas, then stay at work until six weeks before the birth, so I can claim maternity allowance.

November

Although having a baby will mean a lot of problems, in a way I am pleased, as it will give me something to live for and focus on. I hope you will remember what you said once – that whatever I do you'll never be ashamed of me.

Love from Lucy."

It was a colossal cheek, she knew, what she was asking. She was asking them to disrupt their comfortable middle-aged way of life and adjust to a new baby in their house, of whose existence they'd be deeply ashamed. She knew there'd be some hard words spoken but didn't doubt for a moment that they'd accept her. Her father's love for her might be damaged irreparably, but she knew his sense of duty was very strong in family matters.

It was with difficulty that she brought herself to drop the letter in the pillar box on her way to work next morning. Up until now her pregnancy had been a source of joy, but she knew there'd be bitterness in it now that her parents knew.

Next morning she pictured the letter rustling in at the letterbox at home, and dropping on the mat. Her mother would open it absently, not expecting much news. Then she'd read it and her face would change... Dad would be home about half past six that evening. Mum wouldn't tell him at first; she'd let him have his dinner in peace. Then she'd give him the letter... Lucy couldn't bear to think of it.

Of course it was too soon to expect a reply from them next day, or the day after. It came the day after that. Lucy went downstairs to fetch the milk in the morning, and there on the doormat lay the familiar blue envelope with her father's small, firm handwriting.

Lucy trembled as she picked it up, wishing she didn't have to open it. She took it upstairs and started to eat her cornflakes, still unable to open it. Well, she couldn't sit there staring at it. It must be opened. She slit it open and read it fearfully:

"Dear Lucy,

Well, we have got your letter. As you can guess, we don't know what to say. There are so many things to say, and if we didn't say some of them it would be pretending. We're shocked, and sad, and hurt. And dead worried. What do you mean – our standards? Isn't that the only standard? Anything else is chaos.

You've picked a hard road, Lucy. Whatever anyone else says, and when all the dust has settled, you've got a hard road ahead of you. We will help you all we can. We'll be on your side. And you know we mean that. Come home when the time comes.

This a short letter, but you probably don't want a long one. Mum and I have written it together.

All our love Lucy, the same as always,
Mum and Dad."

Lucy wept into her cornflakes, partly in relief and partly emotion. It was a beautiful letter, stern yet kind, no hard words and no words wasted. She felt a new respect for her father, able to write such a letter when he must be deeply upset.

She'd have to write to her brother and grandfather too, but she didn't fear their reactions as much as she feared those of her parents. She wrote both letters that evening.

She had a feeling her grandfather wouldn't take the news too badly, somehow. He'd probably be pleased at becoming a great-grandfather, despite the circumstances. He was a breezy old man who went bumbling around like a big bee, getting on everyone's nerves. Lucy had been fond of him as a child but found him irritating since she'd grown up. But she admired him; he was over eighty and fiercely independent, living in his bungalow on the south coast of Devon when he wasn't really fit to look after himself anymore. He replied to her letter by return of post:

"Dear Lucy,

You know how it feels when your heart seems to drop? Well, that's just how I felt when I read your letter. It was not until I came to the point 'I can't help feeling pleased about it', that I brightened up. I am glad you feel like that, because so do I now. It's not a bit of good thinking and worrying about things that have already happened. It's the future we must look to, and though it seems cloudy with problems, remember you won't be alone in coping with them, we shall all be with you.

I can assure you, Lucy, there will be no prejudice from me, and I shall love him or her as I have always loved you, and be a proud great-grandfather in March.

All my love,
Grandad

PS Don't let this man pester you in any way. He can be stopped."

Lucy laughed out loud at the postscript, but she was very pleased with her grandfather's letter.

She wondered what her brother Jim would say. She had no idea about his moral views, but she knew that some of his friends lived with their girlfriends. His reply to her letter came after a few days:

"Dear Lucy,

This news comes as a great surprise, almost shock. I must admit that my first reaction is to feel sad and disappointed. However, I must say I would very much like to have a nephew or niece, although I never envisaged these circumstances. You say you will bring it up yourself, and I hope this will be possible for you. I am very willing to help you in any way I can, e.g. financially.

As far as the father is concerned, if you are not going to claim maintenance it would be best to have absolutely nothing whatever to do with him again, otherwise he could create some bad emotional problems for you.

I expect you have some difficult problems ahead of you, both financial and social. No doubt you have had a very worrying time. Now that you have settled things to some extent you should do your best not to worry about the future and relax a little.

Well, I am certain that I will love the child as

my nephew or niece, and he or she will always be welcome here for visits.

My very best wishes for the future, and if there is any way in which I can help, please do let me know.

Love from Jim."

She'd never accept any money from him, of course, but it was kind of him to suggest it. But why was he shocked, sad and disappointed? Did certain standards apply to his sister but not to his friends? He'd regarded it as a joke when one of his friends had to get married in a hurry, but obviously he thought such things shouldn't happen in his own family.

*

The silence on the subject at work was broken one morning when Charlie Radlett asked awkwardly, "When are you leaving us, Lucy?"

"Early February."

"Oh. So you... er... I see, yes." He fumbled with some papers, then picked up the telephone for relief in a conversation with someone in another department.

Trying to hide her smile at his embarrassment, Lucy wandered off to get some envelopes from the cabinet.

"You look well today, Lucy," observed Mrs Browning. "Really blooming."

"Do I?" grunted Lucy. "Hmph."

*

"Lucy," Margaret admonished her over coffee that evening. "Why are you so ungracious when people pay you compliments? You really snubbed poor old Mrs Browning this morning. Don't you like compliments?"

"Of course I do. But they embarrass me. I don't know how to reply to them, so I just grunt."

"You are funny, Lucy! You make me laugh!"

Lucy knitted in silence for a while, then she asked curiously, "Why do you like me? I suppose you do, or you wouldn't let me come round so often."

Margaret thought for a minute, then she replied, "I like you because you surprise me. You're not what you seem. I feel in tune with you, we can natter but it doesn't matter if we don't."

"Yes," agreed Lucy. "When you can be silent with someone without feeling awkward it means you're really friends… I wish I had more friends like you. The trouble with me is I'm not really interested in other people. What do we talk about when I'm here? We talk about me! Do I think about myself too much?"

"Well, yes, but probably no more than a lot of people do. We're all basically selfish, and you haven't got any children yet to need you and draw you out of yourself."

"I thought sex would draw me out of myself, but I'm still just as bad as I was before I met Joe. Being a mother might not make me any different, either."

Yet, thought Lucy as she walked back through the dark damp streets, *I hope I'll improve a bit when the baby comes.* Pale fog thickened the air, and Lucy walked carefully. She was just crossing the road when two orbs of light flashed in her eyes, and a car screeched to a halt a few yards away. A window was slammed down, and a raucous female voice rasped, "Bloody silly ass! Can't you look where you're going?"

She drove off, leaving Lucy badly shaken, reflecting on the fragile transience of life…

12

Christmas

Lucy dreaded going home for Christmas. *I've been afraid of Dad all my life*, she realised as she waited at Paddington station, *but I've never been so afraid of him as I am now.*

The porter gave her an odd look as he checked her ticket, which puzzled her until she remembered she was six months pregnant and booked on the train sleeper as "Miss L Grey". *I wish this Women's Lib idea of every woman being Ms would catch on*, thought Lucy. *It would save people like me such awkwardness.*

She was glad she had the sleeper compartment to herself. Not so many people travelled to the West Country this time of year. She felt afraid as the train hurtled through the night. She imagined accidents in the darkness, being killed or losing her baby, trapped in twisted metal wreckage. A year ago, when she'd been so lonely and frustrated, maybe she wouldn't have minded ending it all in a train crash, but now she desperately wanted to live and be a mother.

Eventually the window paled, and Lucy heard birdsong above the rattle of the train. Through the window she glimpsed bare trees etched against the thin pink sky of a winter sunrise. Her fears vanished, and she fell into a doze.

She woke with a start when the train stopped at Penzance. The daylight was cold and unfriendly. Her father was somewhere out there on the station, a terrible judge waiting for her…

There he was, tall and grey, with a sad look in his eyes – not even reproachful – just sad. Lucy tried to smile as she approached him, but it froze on her face.

He took her travel bag, saying, "I'm dead worried about you, Lucy. We'll talk it over with Mum when we get home."

It was awful sitting with him in the bus in such a pregnant silence. Lucy felt like a naughty child awaiting punishment from angry parents. What was her father thinking as he sat there? If only he'd speak, even to reproach her. It would be better than this terrible silence.

It will pass, she told herself. *This moment will pass.* She sometimes found herself able to endure suffering by telling herself that it couldn't go on for ever; it must end sometime. But the worst was still to come.

It came when they entered the house on Palk Road, where her mother greeted her with the same sad, worried expression.

"Sit down, Lucy," said Dad wearily as they entered the sitting room. Mum was in the kitchen making coffee. Lucy sat down, feeling like a convict awaiting their sentence.

"We must be careful what we say," began Dad. "Things said in anger now will be remembered with bitterness later on. But what do you mean when you talk of standards? Aren't our standards yours too?"

"They're the ideal ones."

"They're the only ones. Do you still see this bloke?"

"No."

"I don't want to probe." His voice was disgusted. "It would make me cringe to hear all the details. The rat – if he was here in this room I'd strangle him, crush him. Lower than the lowest form of insect life."

(*Poor Joe*, thought Lucy. *He doesn't deserve that. He's only weak and human, and quite decent really. But of course you see him as the wicked seducer of your daughter.*)

"Why won't you claim maintenance?" demanded Dad fiercely.

"Because of his wife and child," said Lucy faintly.

"All married men are rats," he growled. "They hide behind their wives and children, saying they can't face up to their responsibilities. I've always thought you had common sense, Lucy, and could understand people and situations. You've read books about life. Can't you sum people up? For goodness' sake, don't get sucked in again."

(*Obviously*, thought Lucy, *you see me as a victim. You don't understand that my sexual desire and emotion were stronger than my common sense. It's abhorrent to you that I'd want sex with a man, so you explain it by believing I was made a fool of.*) She sat mute while her father reproached her, but she thought her answers silently.

"You've blasted your life," continued Dad. "From

now on your life is all duty, and any pleasure will only be incidental."

(*Why? Won't having a child be a pleasure, not just a duty? Do married parents regard their children as just duty? I'm no different, except that I have no husband.*)

"That poor kid's not going to have a normal family life like you and Jim had. Have you thought of that? No, I think you're regarding this baby like a doll to play with. A purely selfish attitude."

(*Yes, I am selfish. But maybe no more than lots of mothers who want children for their own pleasure.*)

"And what will you call yourself later on? You'll have to make up some story about being widowed or divorced – for the child's sake. I know moral attitudes are looser nowadays, but the majority of decent people will always feel as we do about such things. Society must protect itself by showing disapproval to people such as you. The world would be in chaos if everyone acted like you've done."

(*Yes, so it would. But most people do marry to have their children, and always will. I've only done it this way because I've never had a chance of marriage.*)

"And what will Mrs Pennick next door tell her two young daughters? Have you thought, in your selfishness, of how this will affect us? All the neighbours and relations we'll have to tell? I don't suppose you have; you've only thought of yourself."

Lucy sat mute. She knew she deserved all this, but had he no mercy, no understanding of human weakness? *No,* she realised, *he's strong, but he's narrow in his strength. He's stern with himself and stern with others, with no charity for those weaker ones.*

Mum came in with the coffee cups and sighed, "Well, Lucy, you've been very irresponsible, to say the least."

Tears welled up in Lucy's eyes. She didn't want to cry; she wanted to remain aloof and silent. But to have both of them going on at her together was too much.

"I'd have thought you'd have enough sense to keep away from married men," remarked Mum. "I always did."

(*Yes, but you weren't still a virgin at twenty-three, with no prospect of a husband.*)

"My mother never told me anything, but I had the sense to keep out of trouble."

(*Ah, but when you were young there weren't the public temptations and enticements to sex that bombard young people nowadays. If I'm a victim at all then I'm a victim of this permissive society.*)

"Don't let it happen again," warned Mum. "I have to say that to you. Men will think you're easy now."

(*There's no need for it to happen again. If I ever have a relationship with a man again it'll only be if it's a genuine, lasting one.*)

"And where are you going to have this baby?"

"Well," choked Lucy through her tears, "I was hoping to have it here at first, just until I can go back to Redfold. But would you mind having a baby here?"

"Yes, I would," replied Mum in a new, hard voice. "But it's the only thing to be done."

Her mother's tone of voice frightened Lucy. It made her realise she couldn't blindly depend on her parents. There were limits.

The telephone rang. It was her brother Jim saying he'd arrive that evening for Christmas.

"Jim's very shocked over this business," observed Dad. "I'm glad he is; it shows he's led a decent life and kept up the Grey standards."

(*Rot! He's shocked because brothers don't expect their sisters to get pregnant, whatever kind of life they and their friends lead themselves.*)

Later Lucy spied a letter in the rack on the cupboard from Jim to her parents. No-one was about just then, so she had a peep at it. He'd written: "*Lucy has been very stupid and weak-willed, and has let the family down, but we must be tolerant and help her all we can.*"

Thank you, Jim, thought Lucy sourly. *Very gracious of you, I'm sure.*

Jim and their grandfather arrived that evening. Jim didn't shake hands with her as he usually did, but Lucy realised it was only because he felt awkward with her in her new situation. Grandad was refreshingly normal with her. His only comment on her condition was, "Well, what's done is done. It's no use going on about it, that's what I say. It's the future we must think of now."

When they were all sitting around the fireside, Lucy felt like a viper in their midst, like a cuckoo in the family nest who'd done something too terrible to be talked about. The baby thumped inside her, and she wanted to run away and hide from their condemning presences.

She was aware of her father regarding her with a sad, disappointed expression. She felt that he still loved her, but not quite the same as before. She knew she'd let him down and caused him much anguish, for which he forgave her but would never forget. *I understand how he feels*, she realised. *If he ran off with another woman I'd be devastated, because he's my father, so I know how he feels now.*

She wondered how her mother felt. It was difficult to tell, as Mum was a reserved woman who didn't display her feelings much. She was knitting a little white jersey. A sob rose in Lucy's throat. How kind of Mum to knit for the baby, when she must be suffering the same anguish as Dad. Lucy wanted to say something to express her gratitude but couldn't.

Jim and Grandad were talking about car insurance and parking meters, while Dad shifted about in his chair, looking bored. Lucy knew he was deeply disappointed at having so little in common with his son. He'd looked forward to long, comradely walks in the hills with his son as he grew up, but Jim wasn't interested in hiking. He liked cars, pubs and parties. Dad was left sad and bewildered – unreasonably so, thought Lucy, for Jim was more normal in the world's eyes than his father. It had been Lucy's lot to inherit many of their father's characteristics. She'd always known that Dad loved her more than Jim.

*

It was Christmas Eve. As a child Lucy used to feel heady with excitement on Christmas Eve, but now she felt stale and heavy as she went to bed. *I wonder what they're saying about me down there in the sitting room now*, she thought bitterly.

She didn't sleep well. She woke up during the night with a heavy, sinister feeling weighing on her, as if she'd woken from a bad dream, though she couldn't recall it. She switched on the bedside light. It seemed hard and unfriendly, as if the room resented the sudden intrusion of artificial light. It was as if the presence of darkness was still there, ready to return in force when the light was switched off. Lucy lay wondering about childbirth, and felt afraid – afraid of pain, and of the unknown. Towards dawn a bird cheeped outside, so faintly that she wasn't sure she'd heard it. Then a blackbird sang, clear and sweet. Lucy switched off the light, and early grey daylight stole in at the window. She slept.

While Lucy helped her mother get the breakfast ready that morning, Mum asked awkwardly, "Is the baby's father young and healthy?"

"Yes, in his thirties," replied Lucy, embarrassed at the mention of him but pleased that her mother obviously cared about the baby's wellbeing.

"Don't tell the neighbours or anyone that he's married," advised Mum. "They might not like it."

Why not? Will they think I'm after their husbands too? thought Lucy with grim humour. *I'm sure I don't fancy bald Mr Pennick!*

All the family gave her gifts of money for Christmas this year. "You'll need every penny you can get from now on," observed Dad grimly.

In the afternoon Lucy wandered down to the beach. It was a mild grey Christmas day, very quiet. The sea lay like a sheet of quicksilver. Lucy strolled across the sand, kicking stones and thinking. *I wish I could share my joy in my pregnancy with the family*, she thought sadly, *but I feel I must pretend to be a contrite, penitent daughter, when really I'm so jubilant inside. I can never do what Dad says and pretend I've been married. I must tell my child the truth about his birth; it's his right to know. If I build up a false story around it he'll think it's something to be ashamed of.*

She watched gulls wheeling and squealing over the slatey sea and felt melancholy. She wished she didn't have to go back home to the house on Palk Road, where they all regarded her with such sad, reproachful eyes. *Well, the worst is over*, she reflected as she walked slowly back up the quiet grey roads. *They've said all they must say now.*

Her father had a few more things to say on the evening before she returned to Redfold.

"Why go back now?" he asked. "You'll be back here again in just over a month; it hardly seems worth it."

"I won't get maternity allowance unless I work up until six weeks before the birth date," explained Lucy. Another reason, of course, was that she wanted to put off coming home for good as long as possible.

"By the time you've paid the train fare back and forwards again there probably won't be much to gain by it," remarked Dad. He rolled a cigarette, and said in a puzzled voice, "You don't seem cast down or worried enough over this business."

"But I'm not," protested Lucy. "Why pretend to feel so if I don't?"

"You ought to feel it and realise that you've got a lot of

work and responsibility ahead of you. It's time you grew up, Lucy, and faced up to life."

He went with her to Penzance station next day. This time Lucy didn't feel sad when the train pulled out. By her disgrace in his eyes, she knew she'd severed some of the cords of affection and fear that had always bound her to her father. Things would never be the same again.

13
Winter

One evening in late January Lucy trudged slowly up Light Street after work. *There's a sort of white quality in the daylight soon after the year's turned*, she reflected, *that tells you spring isn't far off.* Green pins of bulbs sprouted in the gardens, and Lucy's attic was heavily scented with a stout blue hyacinth in full bloom in a pot on the chest of drawers.

She pictured her baby growing and unfolding like a bulb inside her. She watched with wonder as her belly grew fuller, like the base of a white parsnip. *Pregnancy is beautiful*, she reflected. *It's like the words "Thy belly is an heap of wheat" in the Song of Solomon in the Bible.*

She felt a sudden urge to see Joe. She was leaving Redfold next week and wanted to see if he was alright. Also she wanted to ask him about his family and childhood, so she could tell her child about him one day. It was Friday, so she'd go and see if he was playing the piano at the Rat's Castle.

Winter

It was a cold starlit evening as Lucy walked back down Light Street after her tea, but she didn't feel the cold like she used to. Her extra bulk kept her warm. She felt sad as she viewed the twinkling lights of Redfold. She'd grown fond of the town in her two years there and was soon to leave it, not knowing when or if she'd be back.

She crossed the railway bridge and tackled the steep climb up to the Rat's Castle. Piano music floated out on the cold air, but it didn't sound like Joe. She cautiously pushed open the brown glass door and peered around in the dim smoky light, conscious of curious glances from the men and hostile looks from the women. No, it was someone else at the piano, not Joe.

Why doesn't he play there anymore? she wondered as she walked heavily down past the station again. *Maybe his nerves affected his piano playing.* She wished she knew. Sleet started to float down, and the wind shrilled in telegraph wires by the station.

*

On Monday morning Lucy woke up and saw snow on the skylight window. *Oh no*, she thought, *I hope the roads aren't slippery*. There was a soft light blanket of snow on the pavements. *It's a pity to disturb it; it's so beautiful*, reflected Lucy as she walked very carefully down to the bus stop.

Her pregnancy could hardly be ignored in the office now, but no-one asked any awkward questions, just – when was she leaving? Where would she live?

Old Frankie the post messenger had looked but made no comment when her condition became obvious, until one morning last week he'd whispered in a conspiratorial manner, "You'll be leaving us soon, I suppose?"

"Yes, the week after next."

"Eh, dear," sighed Frankie. "It's a shame. He don't wanna know you now, I suppose."

Lucy smiled. To Frankie there were two kinds of women: the bad girls, who wore lots of make-up, very short skirts and "led men on"; and the good girls, who were "decent" and taken advantage of by unscrupulous men. *Obviously I'm one of the good girls in his eyes*, decided Lucy, *because I'm quiet and wear modest clothes.*

"You know what they say," continued Frankie. "It's the good girls what have the babies, and the bad girls what get the fur coats! God bless you, dear, I hope all goes well."

Lucy was pleased and touched at his clumsy kindness. Walking over to the canteen, she saw Mr Roberts in the distance. He'd moved to a different department a few months ago, so she hadn't seen him since. Her heart began to thump, and she felt stiff all over. What would he think? What would he say? He was with another man, so he didn't stop to speak as she passed by, just gave her a nod and a cool, "Hello, Lucy." By his raised eyebrows and mocking look, Lucy could see that his opinion of her was the same as Ruth's – that she'd done something rather stupid.

Lucy's cheeks burned in humiliation as she entered the canteen. Why did people who she wanted to impress – like Ruth and Mr Roberts – have a poor opinion of her, while others whose opinions didn't matter – such as old Frankie

– thought more highly of her? She felt depressed about it all afternoon.

There was a letter for her on Crimmond's hall mat when she got back after work. The envelope was marked "Redfold Poets", and Lucy thumped upstairs in excitement with it. She'd recently sent a poem to a local poetry society, and this letter was such a small thin one that obviously they weren't returning her poem. She tore it open. There was a brief slip inside, accepting and thanking her for the poem. *Success, success at last!* thought Lucy jubilantly, dancing around her attic as lightly as her bulk would allow. *I've actually got something into print! Wonderful!*

It was a short poem she'd written back in the summer on that hot, baking afternoon when she'd gone to look at Joe's house on Pains Road. She looked through her other poems and set aside a few more to send, then remembered that she wouldn't be in Redfold much longer. Well, she'd try some Cornish poetry society.

"Lucy?" called Ruth at the door. "Are you in?"

Lucy hastily stuffed all her papers out of sight, then opened the door.

"I'm not sure when you're leaving," announced Ruth, "so I thought I'd give you this now." She handed Lucy a tissue-wrapped package. It was a set of tiny mittens, hat and jacket, beautifully knitted in fine white wool.

"Thank you very much," stammered Lucy, surprised and touched. "They're lovely. Did you knit them yourself?"

"I did. I'm quite a domesticated person really, you know."

"But they look really professional."

"I am professional!" Ruth laughed. "When's the expected great day?"

"The seventeenth of March."

"Well, I hope it all goes well, and that it's a boy like you want. I knew an illegitimate bloke once. He was quite happy about it, he used to say, 'I was born out of passion, not out of habit!'"

*

Next Tuesday evening Lucy walked over to Blackdown Avenue for the last time.

"It's sad that now I've found a friend like you I've got to lose you," she observed over coffee.

"You won't lose me." Margaret smiled. "You'll be coming back, and we can speak on the phone while you're away. Maybe you'll make some friends while you're at home; it's easier to make friends when you're a mother."

"I hope so. But I'm such a sour, irritable sort of person. I don't seem to like or laugh at the same things most people do."

"Does anything about me irritate you?" asked Margaret.

Lucy thought for a moment, then she replied, "Only the way you carry on about little things sometimes. Once you were telling me about a new schoolchildren's crossing up the road, and you took about ten minutes to tell me!"

"Well, little things like that matter when you're a mother." Margaret laughed.

"Ouch!" exclaimed Lucy, patting her bulk. "He gives a vicious little kick sometimes! It's funny, I feel he and I understand each other, even though he's not born yet. Do you think I'll be a good mother?"

"Yes, if you don't fuss and worry too much over him."

"You know," remarked Lucy, "he hasn't got much good to inherit, really, with an unstable father and a neurotic mother. I'll try to make sure he mixes with other kids from an early age – maybe it'll stop him being shy. Shyness is a curse. If you're shy at sixteen people think you're 'sweet', but if you're shy when you're over twenty they think you're weird."

"Isn't there anything about Joe that you'd like the baby to inherit?" asked Margaret.

"Yes, quite a lot, really," said Lucy thoughtfully. "His gentleness, his kindness, his musical talent. He's a nice person, really, but we didn't have the same sense of humour, and that's hopeless for any relationship. He's been unfortunate in life; he's made for better things than driving vans, but he had to leave school early because his mother was hard up, so he couldn't get qualified at anything."

Margaret disappeared upstairs, returning with a large paper bag. "There, I've finished it in time," she announced, carefully unfolding a white crocheted baby's cape and hood.

"It's beautiful." Lucy held it reverently. "I'll get him christened in it."

All too soon it was time to go. Lucy put on her coat and said sadly, "I'll miss coming round here on Tuesday evenings."

"I'll miss you too. Let me know as soon as the baby comes. I'll be thinking of you, Lucy. Goodbye." She waved

Life *for* Lucy

from her lighted front doorway until Lucy turned the corner.

Lucy walked slowly back through dark wet streets, feeling sad. *That's how life is*, she reflected. *You make friends, you're happy with them, then you lose them and hopefully find new ones. But it doesn't seem possible that I could ever become as close to anyone again as I am with Margaret.*

*

Friday afternoon came. Lucy lingered until all the goodbyes were over and the others had gone. She wandered alone around the grey office room, past dusty filing cabinets, ink-stained desks and tall dingy windows. She didn't feel sad at leaving the place; she hadn't been unhappy there, just neutral… She put the cover over her typewriter for the last time, picked up her bag and the blue baby jacket Mrs Browning had given her, then she left.

She did a little shopping on Saturday morning, then sat in the park for a while before tackling the long, steep climb of Light Street. She sat and admired the grey velvet barks of beech trees, and snowdrops pearling the grass.

She idly watched a father, mother and a little toddler boy walk by. Then she stiffened – the man was Joe. She shrank behind a bush overhanging the end of the bench. He mustn't see her – not with his wife there – it would be disastrous. She pretended to rummage in her basket, glancing furtively at Joe's wife. She was quite pretty, with dark hair framing a rather sad, gentle face. Lucy looked at the little boy and thought, *He's my child's half-brother, how strange!*

Joe and his wife laughed together over something. Their companionship made Lucy feel lonely, but she was relieved to see their relationship was alright. Obviously his wife didn't know. Lucy was glad she'd seen him but wished they'd had a chance to say goodbye. She hoped he might be able to see their child one day.

Monday afternoon came, and a taxi at the front door. Lucy felt emotionally flat as she looked around her attic for the last time. Often, at moments when she'd thought she'd feel deeply, she found she didn't feel much at all, she just felt numb. The emotion came later. She'd been happy in her attic, on the whole. She loved the faded pink roses on the wallpaper, the chipped enamel sink and skylight window where she could look out and be high up among the chimneys and rooftops. She wished she didn't have to leave.

Lucy followed the taxi man as he lumbered downstairs with her bags. In watery winter sunlight she descended Crimmond's wide stone steps for the last time. She still felt numb inside as she sat in the train up to London. Fields stretched pale green in the late afternoon sunshine. Woods lay soft dark grey, with a touch of purple in them, like mole's fur. Elms spread in webs of grey lace against the sky. Then the sun set in chill crimson streaks, and lights began to wink in the dusk.

Lucy had booked her train sleeper in the name "Mrs L Grey" this time. She despised herself for it, but didn't have the nerve to stand there – vastly pregnant – and label herself "Miss".

There was a finality in buying a single ticket to Penzance, not a return one as usual. She was disappointed at having to share the sleeper compartment. Her companion was a motherly middle-aged woman who told Lucy all about her four children.

"And is your husband pleased?" she asked, glancing at Lucy's bulk.

"I haven't got one," replied Lucy curtly.

The woman looked rather taken aback, then remarked, "Well, never mind."

"I don't."

Lucy watched with relief as the woman's feet, clad in hairy brown bed socks, disappeared up the ladder to the top bunk. She'd very gallantly let Lucy have the bottom one.

Lucy slept better than she usually did on these trains. She was so used to being pregnant by now that she no longer feared accidents or miscarriage. It seemed that she would be pregnant for ever.

The train pulled into Penzance early next morning. Lucy felt a depressing finality: the gates of home were closing in on her, and it might be a long time before she'd be free and independent of her parents again.

14

Spring

One morning in early April Lucy sat up in her hospital bed, trying to concentrate on the book she was reading. The baby was two weeks overdue, so she'd had to come into hospital to have the labour induced.

She gave up reading and looked around her. The ward was bright and cheerful, with blue-flowered curtains and bedspreads. Two women in opposite beds were talking together, and Lucy heard one of them say, "My little horror's down in the nursery."

Lucy felt a sense of shock that any woman could speak of her new-born baby like that. *The novelty must wear off after the first*, she reflected, *but even if I'd given birth to six children I'm sure I couldn't speak so of the seventh.*

A large black nurse approached her and announced curtly, "Injection in your bottom."

Lucy obediently turned over as the nurse drew the

curtains. *How completely one has to put oneself into other people's hands when in hospital*, she thought ruefully. She jumped when the needle jabbed, and the nurse laughed. "Well, I warned you!"

Lucy glanced at the girl in the next bed, wondering whether or not to speak. She caught her eye and the girl nodded listlessly. She seemed quite depressed. Her eye wandered to Lucy's left hand (Lucy was used to people glancing at her wedding finger to see if she was married or not), and the girl looked at her curiously.

"Hello," she said in an Irish voice. "Your first one?"

"Yes."

"Me too." She hesitated, then queried, "Can I ask you something? Are you married?"

"No."

"Neither am I," replied the girl. "They call me Mrs O'Connell here, but I'm really Miss. My name is Nuala, by the way."

"I'm Lucy. They call me Mrs Grey too. It makes me feel a hypocrite, but I suppose they think it's necessary."

"Are you keeping your baby?"

"Yes."

"I'm not. I'd like to, but I can't. I tried everything to get rid of it – hot baths, gin, falling downstairs, but nothing worked."

"Couldn't you get an abortion?"

"Of course not." Nuala looked shocked. "It's against my religion."

Lucy wondered what the moral difference was between aborting oneself and getting someone else to do it.

Spring

"I'm getting married in August," continued Nuala, "to the baby's father back home."

"Then it'll be alright, won't it?" Lucy was surprised. "If you keep the baby?"

"No, I couldn't. My parents – and my boyfriend's parents – would never accept me if they knew I'd had a baby before we were married. I live in a little village near Cork, where everyone knows everything about each other. My family would never live down the shame and disgrace."

"But that's tragic!" exclaimed Lucy, actually moved – for once – by another's trouble. "Are you to be deprived of your child, and it deprived of you, just so your family's pride won't be hurt? They're not worthy to be your parents if they'll only accept you when you conform to their standards."

Nuala looked startled, and Lucy wondered if she'd spoken too strongly.

Just then a nurse approached, drew the bed curtains, removed Lucy's nightdress and put a white cotton gown on her. She felt apprehensive as she was wheeled on a trolley into a little room with a huge light in the ceiling.

"Good morning, Mrs Grey," said a breezy young doctor. "We're going to get that baby started on its way."

Lucy let her legs be strapped up, and the doctor poked about with various instruments under the harsh light. She cried out in pain when what felt like an egg-beater was inserted inside her, then she told herself: *It will pass; the pain will pass.* She made herself relax and was able to bear it.

"I felt a little hand then," observed the doctor. "It's a big baby."

His face looked very large to Lucy under the light, but she felt reassured by his competent manner and trusted him to deliver her safely of her baby. He injected her arm with a needle attached to a plastic tube and bottle, which contraption seemed to be permanent for the next few hours after she was wheeled back to the ward. Nuala had disappeared, and Lucy wondered how things were going for her. She hoped she'd decide to keep her baby after all.

Lucy felt drowsy. She became aware of heavy, dragging sensations in her abdomen, like a weight pressing on her. They were familiar, as she'd occasionally experienced period pains similar to these. She felt reassured, thinking, *Well, if this is what labour pains are like, then I've nothing to fear, for I know all about it.*

She was wheeled into a dim little room, where she lost all sense of time. She vaguely realised it was dark through the high-up window, so it must be night-time. By breathing deeply she was just about able to bear the contractions, and called on God to help her. Then she laughed as she recalled a quotation she'd read somewhere: "Many people regard God as a pilot regards his parachute – it's there in case of emergency, but he hopes he won't have to use it."

Did God condemn her for unlawfully bringing forth this new life? What was it Christ had said to the woman caught in adultery? "Neither do I condemn thee. Go, and sin no more."

Lucy didn't feel like an "unmarried mother" – she was just a mother, and it seemed quite natural. She'd felt annoyed when Aunt Ethel wrote to her, "*Your mother has told me of your misfortune, and I am sorry it has happened to you."* How could anyone regard the birth of her baby as a misfortune? Yet the world did, she knew.

She felt a sudden urge to push and assumed she needed to empty her bowels. *Odd*, she thought, *I had an enema this morning*. She called the nurse and asked for a bedpan. The big black nurse who'd given her an injection that morning took one look at Lucy and announced briskly, "It's not a bedpan you want, my girl!" then wheeled her into the delivery room.

Lucy was alarmed. This was the part she dreaded – the baby pushing its head out. The room was starkly lit by a strip-light in the ceiling, and Lucy looked around for the doctor. She thought doctors always delivered babies, but there was only the nurse and a young midwife. She felt afraid when they left the room for a moment – afraid that she'd be left to give birth alone. They soon came back, and Lucy felt primeval as she screwed up her face and uttered animal grunts of extreme effort.

"Push, Mrs Grey, push!" encouraged the nurse. "You're doing fine, I can see the baby's head coming."

The midwife gave her a quick injection and made a cut in the birth canal entrance. Just as Lucy felt stretched beyond endurance she heard them exclaiming that the baby was out. She was surprised at it being born so quietly; she'd expected it to struggle and screech. She saw them lift the yielding, elastic little body, which gave a whimper.

"Is it a boy?" asked Lucy.

"Yes," replied the nurse. "You have a son, Mrs Grey."

Lucy sank back, satisfied. Of course it was a boy; there was no need to ask. They weighed him, wrapped him in a blanket and laid him on the pillow beside his mother.

"Here's your son, Mrs Grey." The nurse beamed. "All nine pounds of him!"

He lay on the pillow beside her, his hair matted with her blood, regarding her wisely and curiously with bright, dark blue-grey eyes. Lucy gazed at him with wonder, amazed that she'd actually conceived, carried and given birth to this live little creature.

"Five o'clock in the morning," announced the nurse for Lucy's benefit. It was the third of April. She acquiesced when the nurse took the baby away to be bathed; he seemed more the hospital's property than hers at the moment. But she made sure she saw the midwife fix a plastic label around his wrist with the name "SAMUEL GREY".

Things were done to her again. She was washed, strapped up, stitched up, all in a haze of happiness and relief. Then she was wheeled back to the ward.

Morning sunlight streamed in at the windows. Lucy turned to look out of the window behind her bed. The hospital seemed to have spacious grounds. She saw a chestnut tree with a veil of golden buds, and hawthorns spattered with green. Everything was young and fresh and new-born, like her baby.

She lay quietly happy for a while, then shuddered as she heard distant cries of agony from the labour room. Someone was having a bad time.

"What a fuss some people make over their labour pains," she heard one of the new young mothers remark contemptuously. "There's nothing to scream about in having a baby; I hardly knew I was having mine."

Lucy felt sad and angry. Didn't people understand

that what was easy for them could be difficult for others? Could compassion only be learned through suffering? Would the strong always sneer at the weak? *No*, she told herself, *think of Margaret: she's strong, yet her compassion and understanding of life are profound.*

Someone pulled back the curtain of the next bed, and Lucy realised that Nuala was there.

"Hello," she greeted Lucy. "Have you had yours?"

"Yes," replied Lucy. "I've had a boy."

"I've had a girl," said Nuala proudly, "and I'm keeping her. I can't bear to give her away; she's so lovely. I'll tell my boyfriend and we'll get married here, then when we go back to Ireland we'll tell our families we've adopted her."

"But suppose they see that she looks like you?"

"She's got her Dadda's red hair!" Nuala giggled. "But it'll be alright…"

Lucy hoped so. She saw a nurse coming towards her with a little bundle – a baby wrapped in a blanket.

"Your mother rang up, Mrs Grey," announced the nurse. "She's pleased to hear you've got such a big baby boy. Here he is." She placed the firm, warm bundle in Lucy's arms. "Do you want to breastfeed?"

"Yes, of course." Lucy felt clumsy trying to hold up his head, which drooped heavily. She wondered if she had any milk to give him yet.

"Give your nipple a good hard squeeze," advised the nurse. "There should be some colostrum in there now."

Lucy did so, and was amazed and delighted to see a little cream bead of milk curl out. It seemed a miracle that she had life-giving fluid in her breasts to feed and nourish her baby. She winced as he sucked strongly. It was painful, but somehow she welcomed the pain and felt a fierce pride in this strong little male child she'd produced out of her body. She still regarded him more with wonder than with love, but she knew the love would blossom as she grew to know him.

Her arms ached and thrilled with tenderness for this warm little being suckling for his life, utterly dependent on her. She wanted to give, give, give to him – give her milk, her strength, herself... *God is infinitely clever*, she reflected. *He's caused me to bear this child, and now He's going to plant this thing called mother-love in me to make sure I feed and rear him as best I can.*

Little Samuel regarded her blankly while he suckled. No, his eyes weren't blank; they were like clean slates on which life hasn't written yet. *He'll get hurt one day*, thought Lucy, *and there's nothing I can do to prevent it. All I can give him is love and a little learning, and just hope the world won't be too unkind to him. Poor little cuss! He's got to grow up and learn to cope with people and get disillusioned and disappointed... I hope he won't find it all so difficult as I do.*

His sucks grew less powerful, and he slept. Lucy felt a deep sense of satisfaction. She'd gone through every natural physical experience a woman can have: intercourse, pregnancy, childbirth and breastfeeding.

She looked down at the warm, live little boy asleep in her arms. Little Samuel Grey. He was beautiful... Lucy gazed at him, and knew that – though there'd be problems and maybe hard times ahead – life would never seem empty or futile again.

15
Forty Years On

No, life for Lucy was never empty or futile again, though it was hard at times. She never went back to Redfold, apart from occasional visits to Margaret.

One summer evening forty years later, Lucy was sitting in the garden of her grandfather's bungalow in Devon, looking out over the sea. Grandad had bequeathed his bungalow to Lucy when he'd died, soon after which – much to her surprise – she got married!

After five difficult years living with her parents and Samuel, Lucy met Bernard through a postal writing club, where they became penfriends, falling in love by letters. He was quite a lot older than her, but they were like twin souls on paper. When they met up at last, they found it very hard to communicate by speech, because they weren't used to it. They were like a couple of strangers, even though they knew each other so well on paper. Eventually they managed to thaw out and get married, realising that they were each other's last chance, but neither of them ever found the person they'd fallen in love with on paper.

It hadn't been too bad, reflected Lucy. *He was kind, he adopted Sam, he gave me a good life and a lovely daughter.* Their daughter Morwenna was born a couple of years into their marriage. Now Morwenna lived and worked as a teacher in London, coming home to visit in school holidays.

Lucy was a widow by now, happily living alone, pottering around in her bungalow and writing her books. She'd found her genre in writing children's fantasy books, which she published herself with the help of money she'd inherited from her share of the sale of her parents' house after they'd died. She'd sold quite a few through advertising them.

Sam was married by now, with a family, living a couple of miles away near a shop where he sold and repaired bicycles. He hadn't fulfilled his mother's dream of turning out to be a famous author or musician; his creative talents were more in the line of mechanics. But he was a pleasant, honest, hardworking young man (well, at forty he still seemed young to Lucy!), and she knew that was what really mattered. She'd told him about Joe when he was old enough to understand.

Gazing out at the sunset glowing orange over the sea, Lucy cast her mind back thirteen years when Sam had dropped a bombshell – he'd met his father!

"I went to Redfold last weekend," he announced on one of his visits, "to number 12 Pains Road."

Lucy's heart jumped. She'd never told him Joe's address. "But how…?" she gasped.

"I found Joseph Broome on the electoral register," explained Sam. "I had to drive to Portsmouth to pick up some special bike parts, so it wasn't too far from there to Redfold. I found a bed and breakfast place to stay at, then next morning I went to Pains Road."

"Did you see him?" asked Lucy faintly.

"Yes, but I was careful," Sam assured her. "I thought I'd better not knock on the door in case his wife answered, as I might look like him. A neighbour was painting a fence next door, so I asked him, 'Does Joe Broome live there at number 12?' He said yes, he does, so I asked, 'Can you knock on his door and tell him someone wants to speak to him?' He did, then Joe answered the door. I stood on the other side of the road, so he came over to me there."

"What did he look like? He'll be over sixty by now."

"He had white hair," replied Sam. "I asked him, 'Do you remember Lucy Grey?' He said yes, so I told him, 'I'm her son. I was born in 1971.' He looked a bit shocked and said, 'So you're… you're my son… I think we'd better go somewhere and talk – there's a café up the road.' So we went to this little working men's café and talked."

"What did he say?" asked Lucy eagerly. "I wish I'd been a fly on the wall!"

"I told him I've got a step-dad and a sister, and that I run a bike shop. He told me he'd had to give up work because of short-term memory loss. I forgot to ask about my half-brother. I told him you didn't know I was there.

At first he kept asking me, 'What do you want?' as if he thought I was going to blackmail him."

"I bet he did." Lucy smiled grimly. "He must have been so scared that the past had caught up with him at last. What else did he say?"

"Well… we just talked man chat about bikes and stuff. I liked him; I think he'd have been a good dad."

This was a dig at Lucy's husband Bernard, as he and Sam had never liked each other.

Lucy wished that Sam could recall more about his meeting with his father. She'd like to have asked if Joe had said much about her but felt awkward asking Sam that…

*

Still sitting in her garden, Lucy watched the crimson circle of sun sink into the sea, then she went indoors.

A few days later, Sam dropped another bombshell – he'd found his half-brother Roland on the internet. "He lives in Portsmouth," he told Lucy. "He's a local DJ in his spare time; I've found his website."

Lucy looked up the website of Roland Broome, and saw his picture… Her heart turned over. There was something about him that she recognised; he was like Joe yet not like Joe. Memories of the past came flooding back…

"I'm going to send Roland an email and tell him I'm his brother," declared Sam next time she saw him.

He wasn't prepared for the angry response. Roland thought it was an internet scam and refused to believe him. *Well, I don't blame him*, thought Lucy, after reading his email that Sam had forwarded to her. *I wouldn't believe someone who said my dad was their father. I'd better contact him myself and tell him the whole story.* She opened her laptop, went to her email page, and began to type:

"Dear Roland,

I'm sorry you got such a shock when my son Samuel contacted you. I will explain how he is your half-brother. My name is Lucy, and I met your father at a party in Redfold in 1970. At first he didn't tell me he was married, but then he told me quite early in our acquaintance, giving me a chance to back out... but I didn't, because I liked him and found him very attractive. At twenty-three I was shy and lonely and had never had a boyfriend, so I welcomed this chance of romance, with no thought of any future.

Joe felt very guilty deceiving your mother. He never stopped loving her, but she was so busy with you when you were a baby, and often very tired, so she didn't have much time left for Joe, and he got frustrated. He never meant to be unfaithful; he just let it happen when he met me.

When I became pregnant, he was absolutely horrified, and very frightened. His father-in-law owned the house where you lived on Pains Road, so he had a lot to lose if your mother had found out about me. But she never did find out, because I never told her. It could have destroyed your family if I had, and he couldn't afford to pay me maintenance anyway. I was pleased to be having a baby, really; it gave me something to live for. Joe thought he'd done me a terrible wrong, but I didn't see it like that. My son Samuel was born in April 1971.

What I am telling you is the absolute truth. If you don't believe me, I have a letter your father wrote to me in 1970, which I can photocopy and post to your address on your website. But don't tell your mother about all this; it would hurt and upset her. I never intended to tell you, but now that Sam has contacted you, you need to know the whole story.

Please forgive me for dropping such a bombshell on you. I'm the woman who had an affair with your father behind your mother's back, so you have every right to be angry with me. But please don't be angry with Sam; he's the innocent outcome of this affair, and I'm sure you'd like him if you met him. He's a nice bloke, like your dad. Joe was a nice, kind, decent man, and that's how I remember him.

With all good wishes,
Lucy Parr."

Roland sent back a curt reply:

"As I'm sure you can imagine, I find this to be shocking, to say the least. I would like to see proof of your claim, and would appreciate it if you could send me a copy of the letter you say my father wrote to you, plus a photo of Samuel, and a copy of his birth certificate showing the father's name."

So Lucy replied:

> "I understand your shock and anger, I would be shocked too if someone turned up claiming to have had a child by my father. I am posting you some copies of photos of Sam as a toddler, when he looked very much like his father. I am also sending you a copy of the letter your father wrote to me. There is no need to send you a copy of Sam's birth certificate, because to protect Joe's identity I did not tell it to the registrar, so there is a line drawn through the blank space where the father's name should be. I am very sorry to have upset you, and you need not hear from me again."

After having a long conversation with Sam on the telephone, Roland softened a bit, and sent Lucy another email:

> "Thank you in advance for sending copies of photos and letter. We just want to check family resemblance and Dad's handwriting. Having spoken to Sam at length on the phone, the whole situation is becoming more believable. Dad passed away suddenly last year after a short illness. He desperately wanted to tell me something shortly before he died, but I didn't get the opportunity to speak to him alone before he passed away. We presume this is what he wanted to tell me.
>
> As you can imagine, this has come as a

tremendous shock, and we need time to come to terms with the situation.
Kind regards,
Roland."

Lucy wondered who he meant by "we", and replied:

"Thank you for your kind reply. When you say 'we', do you mean yourself and your mother? I was hoping you wouldn't tell her about all this, as it would cause her so much hurt."

His reply came:

"By 'we' I mean my wife and I."

A few days later a letter dropped onto Lucy's front doormat. The envelope was written in a hand she didn't recognise, so she opened it curiously. There was a handwritten letter inside, and glancing at the end of it, she saw it was signed with the name Rosemary Broome. Her heart gave a great thump. So Roland *had* told his mother! She began to read the letter fearfully:

"Dear Lucy,
I am Rosemary, Joe's wife. I feel so ashamed of his behaviour to you, the shabby way you were treated all those years ago. He went out and seduced a vulnerable young girl out of selfishness, not even taking proper precautions – unforgiveable. I'm sure

you love your son Samuel, but supposing you had been left with a baby you did not want? Not to mention he let me down too. I had a bad time giving birth to Roland and was undergoing treatment for a long time afterwards. I don't suppose Joe told you that. He did hint that he might have to get his needs met elsewhere, but silly me did not think he would do it!

I can see now why he was in such a state at the time of your pregnancy; I wondered what on earth had made him like that. He tried to carry on at work but was unable to think what he was doing; he just left. I had to get someone from DHSS to sort us out something to live on while he went to the day care unit at the local psychiatric hospital.

Unfortunately Joe had a dark side in the form of a bad temper, which I did not know about before I married him. He would often shout and argue and upset me over nothing, even when I was pregnant. He hit me sometimes, causing bad bruising. Even the poor old cat was violently flung to the floor if it sat in his chair.

I will not shock you any more with all the things which happened during our marriage. He was kind and loving in between these episodes, and later he was diagnosed as suffering from paranoid schizophrenia. About twenty years ago he began to experience strange turns when he did not know what he was doing, even pulling off my shoes at a family funeral! He had to retire from work early due to short-term memory problems; sometimes he couldn't find his way home, and once he asked me who I was.

In the end he died aged seventy-three from lung disease plus cancer of the oesophagus, probably caused by smoking all his life. He got quite fat in later years, but the cancer made him unable to swallow, so he starved to death. A tragic end. After he died I moved to a flat in Portsmouth, to be near Roland.

Anyway, I'm pleased that Roland and Samuel turned out so well.

Sincerely,

Rosemary Broome."

Lucy was so pleased and touched by this letter, that there were tears in her eyes. How kind and forgiving of this woman to write such a letter to the woman who'd committed adultery with her husband! Lucy wrote a letter back immediately, apologising for the past and asking Rosemary to forgive her.

After that they wrote letters regularly, and Rosemary sent copies of family photographs "for Sam's interest in his relatives". Lucy was shocked to see a photo of Joe in his seventies, shortly before he died. *Old age can be an absolute obscenity*, she reflected, gazing sadly at the fat old man with bald head, piggy eyes, bulbous nose and sunken mouth. Looking at his younger photos, she could see why she'd fallen for him all those years ago…

She could also see what her life would have been like if he'd been free and had married her. The revelations in

Rosemary's first letter had shocked and surprised her. She found it hard to believe that Joe could be violent. *But of course*, she reflected, *you don't know what someone's really like until you're married and living with them.*

One of the photos showed Rosemary and Roland as a little boy, sitting in the back yard of a brown brick house, obviously Pains Road. If Lucy had married him, she'd have been stuck in a dingy little terraced house like that for years, with a feckless, temperamental husband who'd have been exasperated with her quiet, introverted personality – and would have let her know it violently! There'd have been people in and out of the house all the time, as he'd had a big extended family of siblings and cousins who were always visiting. Lucy shuddered... it would have been *awful!*

She came to the conclusion that quality of life matters more than romance, which is so fleeting. After a brief romance with Joe, there'd have been years of hard graft of marriage in a dreary place. They wouldn't have been able to move to her grandfather's bungalow, because Joe had to be near his job, and he wouldn't have wanted to leave all his relatives anyway.

I did much better with Bernard, realised Lucy with a wry smile, *even though he was about as romantic as a rice pudding...*

Her father's gloomy prediction had been wrong – there *had* been plenty of pleasure in her life; it *hadn't* been all just duty. She'd never regained the companionable relationship she'd had with her father when young, and had shed no tears when he died.

Recently her brother Jim had been doing some family tree research, discovering that their grandparents had married only four months before their father was born. *So that's why Grandad was so kind when I was pregnant,* realised Lucy. *So much for what Dad called the "Grey standards"! I wonder if he ever found out? He'd have been absolutely horrified!*

Then one day Sam announced, "I'm going to meet up with Roland in Portsmouth next week. How about you coming too, to meet his mum?"

"But Roland won't want to see me," protested Lucy. "He won't want to meet the woman who had an affair with his dad!"

"Well, he needn't," suggested Sam. "I can drop you off somewhere to meet his mum, then pick you up later."

Lucy mulled this over. She would like to meet Rosemary but wasn't sure whether Rosemary would want to meet her. They'd never suggested phoning each other, so she wrote a quick letter to tell her about Sam and Roland meeting up, and would Rosemary like to see her too?

Yes, she would, came back the answer by return of post, with a phone number to ring to arrange it. Lucy wondered what time would be best to phone, eventually deciding on 7:30 in the evening.

"Hello?" came a hesitant voice on the line.

"It's Lucy here," she stammered, "about meeting up."

"Oh, yes." Rosemary's voice was quiet and gentle, with a refreshing common touch. Lucy realised with relief that she need not be afraid of her. They arranged to meet by

Portsmouth Guildhall, where Rosemary said she'd be carrying a pink wicker basket, so Lucy could recognise her.

*

It was a hot midsummer morning when Sam and Lucy started out on the long drive to Portsmouth. After being up so early, Lucy fell asleep along the motorway. She woke with a start when Sam announced, "Nearly there."

Soon they approached the large grey Guildhall, where Lucy spied a little dark-haired lady in a cream blouse and trousers. She'd have known her anyway, without the pink wicker basket, from the photos she'd sent. They got out of the car and approached her.

"Hello, Lucy." She smiled. "Hello, Sam."

"I can't stay long," explained Sam, "or a traffic warden will catch me. But it's nice to meet you."

They all shook hands, and Rosemary gave Sam a searching look. "You're so much like your father," she observed.

"Am I?" Sam looked pleased. "I must go now. I'll pick you up at five o'clock," he told his mother, then went off to meet his brother Roland.

Lucy and Rosemary smiled shyly at each other. "Let's go for a walk in the park," suggested Rosemary. Her careworn face still had traces of past prettiness, but her dark hair was obviously dyed.

They strolled through Victoria Park behind the Guildhall and sat down on a bench to talk.

"I'm so sorry about what happened forty years ago," began Lucy.

"No, that's alright," Rosemary assured her. "It's him I'm angry with, not you. He shouldn't have deceived me like that."

"Didn't you ever suspect anything?" asked Lucy. "I don't understand how he could have acted normal, as if nothing had happened, after being out with me."

"Oh, men are like that." Rosemary gave a bitter laugh. "They put things into compartments. I had no idea he was being unfaithful, but I wondered what on earth was wrong when he had the breakdown."

"Would you have divorced him if you'd known about me?"

"I don't know, really; I was a bit more feisty then. But I don't think he'd have coped if I'd divorced him; he was in such a state with the breakdown. I expect he'd have persuaded me to stay with him, and there was Roly to consider. Roly's very angry with his dad over this – he doesn't put flowers on his grave anymore."

"I asked him not to tell you, in the email I sent him."

"He wanted me to say it wasn't true," explained Rosemary. "But I wasn't surprised, really, when he told me what he'd heard from you. Once Joe told me about what his doctor had said, that he'd go off and have affairs when his wife was indisposed. I thought it most inappropriate for a doctor to say that, but I never dreamt that Joe was taking it as a green light to do the same thing!"

They walked down to the Dockyard, where they had fish and chips in a waterside café.

"Did Joe ever say anything about me?" asked Rosemary a bit diffidently.

"He always spoke very highly of you," replied Lucy truthfully. "He said you were the sweetest person in the world, and perfect for him in every way."

"Hmph, he didn't always act like it," muttered Rosemary. "You know, all this clears up a mystery. When Joe was in hospital, he phoned Roly and said, 'Roly, there's something I've gotta tell you, but I must see you on your own.' Roly couldn't get there that day, and by the time he got there next day, Joe was much worse and couldn't speak. He died the day after that."

Lucy munched her chips thoughtfully. So it was still on his conscience, after forty years. He must have spent the rest of his life looking over his shoulder for the past to catch up with him, wondering and worrying that his secret would come to light.

"He would probably have told Roland not to tell you," she mused. "Then you and I would never have met, and you wouldn't have sent me all those photos, and told me all about Joe's life and family so I can tell Sam about his father. I wonder whether Roland would have tried to find Sam if he'd known?"

"Maybe, though he wouldn't have known where to look for him."

After lunch they went up the Spinnaker Tower, where Lucy marvelled at the magnificent views over the Isle of Wight. Turning to the west side, she looked out towards her home in the distant blue haze across Hampshire and Dorset to Devon.

Then they strolled along the seafront to Southsea Common, and back to the Guildhall Square.

"I'm so pleased we've met each other," said Lucy sincerely, "and thank you for everything, for being so kind and forgiving."

"You're very welcome." Rosemary smiled. "Let's carry on writing to each other; I like writing letters."

"So do I," agreed Lucy, as she saw Sam's car come into view. "Goodbye, and thank you."

"Goodbye, Lucy." Rosemary gave her a quick hug, then stood there waving from the steps. Lucy waved back until they were out of sight.

Sam had enjoyed his meeting with Roland; they'd liked each other and found they were quite similar in many ways.

*

Next day Lucy told Margaret all about her trip to Portsmouth in their monthly phone call.

"It's like some story out of *Long Lost Family* on TV," observed Margaret. "You could write a book about it."

"Could I?" wondered Lucy as she walked along the beach later on, looking up at the red earth cliffs that she loved. The tide was out, so she paddled along the wet sand on the shoreline, thinking about and planning her story.

She still had all the diaries she'd written back in those days, so she could use them as a basis for the story. What could she call herself? Claire, that was a name she'd always liked, and she felt that it suited her.

Back in her bungalow, Lucy opened the folder of scrap paper she kept for writing, picked up a pen, and began to write:

"One windy day in March, Claire climbed up the steep rise of Bright Street…"